ROCK STAR

IN THE HEART OF TEXAS BOOK 1

KC KLEIN

Rock Star

In The Heart of Texas Series
Book One

KC Klein

This book is dedicated to my loving parents. Thank you so much for supporting my writing by providing a writer's retreat, a bottle of wine, and in most cases, both.

ONE

"*A*n Abusive lover?"

"Total lie."

"Cheap?"

Brent raised a shoulder. "Super models are expensive. I was going broke."

"Narcissist?"

"Aren't all rock legends?" Brent shot back. The table between them was a bit sticky and the beer in his bottle a bit warm, but the bar was dark and crowded, giving Brent a much-needed sense of normalcy.

But his friend wasn't done teasing him about the latest article the gossip site had posted about him. Derrek looked up from his phone that he was reading from. "You're going with *legend* now, huh? Well, what about her complaints about your small dick?"

Brent tried hard to keep the smile from his lips. "If one considers twelve inches small."

Derrek bit back a laugh. "Only in your dreams, friend. Only in your dreams." He scrolled a little more on his phone. "Okay, okay, this one's actually in the article...how about, cheating man-whore?"

This time his grin turned sheepish. "That may be open to interpretation."

Derrek winced, finally putting down his phone from where he'd been reading off the long list of insults Brent's ex-girlfriend had sold to the gossip magazine about her tumultuous love affair with the famed country music star, aka Brent Kane. "Was that why she broke your nose?"

It was Brent's turn to wince; his nose still hurt. "Now, that one wasn't her fault. My face just got in the way of the wine bottle she'd been throwing."

Derrek, his best friend since elementary school, shook his head. "Let me ask you, do you go looking for crazy...or do the crazies just find you?"

Brent laughed. It was good to be home. Good to be back in the one place he'd actually lived for more than a year. Good to feel his roots again. Funny, when he was a kid he thought nothing ever happened in the small town of Somewhere, Texas, but now, ten years since his last visit, he could see how things had changed.

Sure, there were the old-timers and the regulars, but the kids he'd gone to high school with had grown up; some even had kids of their own. The popularity of the University had increased jobs, and more families had moved into town. When Derek told him they needed to get to Everyday Joe's early to get a table, he'd been shocked. The last time he'd been here, it was just a local dive, and getting a seat was never in question. Hell, by the looks of the rowdy crowd tonight, maybe Joe could afford some decent beer on tap.

Brent slouched down in the booth and raised his bottle to Derrek. "It will be good to get out of the lime light for a while. Let things cool down," he said, then took a sip of his beer and made a face.

Derrek smiled. "Beer still sucks."

Brent nodded. "I mean, seriously... it's a damn bar. With only two things on the menu—beer and fried food—you'd think Joe would give a crap."

Derrek shrugged in that everything-rolls-off-my-back way of his, and sipped from his own bottle. "Cheap beer always wins with college students, but crappy beer aside, I'm glad you're here. Being on the road constantly must be tough. There are times I've felt sorry for you."

Brent hid a grin. Derrek was probably the only person in the world who would feel sorry for him. As a country singer who'd successfully crossed over into pop music, whose recordings had gone multi-platinum, and who'd been on a world tour for the last two years, he pretty much had the jet-set life style people dreamt about. But seven years of working in Nashville and the last two out in L.A. could take its toll on anyone. That was why he'd flown back home, back to the small town of Somewhere, Texas—to take a breather.

"So, do you want to talk about it?" Derrek's voice turned serious while his gaze darted around the crowded bar as if counting the exits for a fast get-away.

They may have known each other most of their lives, but that didn't mean Derrek was comfortable with heart-to-heart conversations. Just not part of the man code. But Brent had already confided in Derrek what his real reasons for getting out of L.A. were.

Along with the rock star lifestyle came the rock star-seeking ladies, and Brent was definitely on their radar. Most of the time, things went smoothly. Well, smooth until the break up.

The problem was that Brent loved the idea of falling in love. The first glance, the first kiss, the first... everything. Brent was into women like some men were into sports cars, but just like a new car smell would eventually fade, so would his desire to be tied down. Of course, the trading-in process wasn't as easy, and sometimes ended badly, like it had with the obsessed super-model, who'd splashed their break-up story across every major gossip magazine.

The whole thing had escalated to the point that he couldn't even leave his front door without being mobbed by reporters. With his latest album not performing as well as he'd hoped, his agent and manager were pressuring him more than ever to write and record his next single. It hadn't helped matters that he now had the worst case of writer's block he'd ever experienced. He'd finally called "uncle" and reached out to his best friend for help. The offer to stay at Derrek's ranch had been a godsend. He needed a place to lay low and get back to what was most important—his music.

Brent shook his head, declining the offer to rehash his problems. He just needed some time to let things blow over. He knew that both of them had crashed and burned in the relationship department, so Derrek was probably not the best person to offer advice.

Derrek looked relieved. "So, what are you planning for the week that you're here?"

Brent rested his head on the vinyl back of the booth and took in the scents of french fries and leather. "A little R and R, write some new material, maybe flirt with a pretty girl."

Derrek raised one eyebrow. "Really? The reason you're here, lying low, is because of a pretty girl."

Brent shook his head. "I write my best material when I'm in love—a little drinking, a little dancing, and a whole lot of tickle between the sheets. The best part about being here is that I'll be gone before the first blush is even off the rose. You remember how that goes—or are you becoming too much of an old man to play that game?"

Derrek laughed and eased his tall frame further into the booth. His height he'd gotten from his father, but his dark Hispanic looks came from his mother's side. "That was all you, man. You're the one who had the way with the ladies. I've never seen anything like it. All you had to do was walk into a room and they would flock to you like flies to road kill."

"You know what your problem is?" Brent continued, as if he had all his crap together and doling out advice to Derrek wasn't at all hypocritical. "You never learned how to talk to women. You always played the silent, brooding type. Sure, some gals dig that, but most like a man who can sweet talk them and tell them they're pretty."

"Silent brooding type, huh?" Derrek said, brows arching above a pair of blue eyes—another trait from his father. But then Derrek just shook his head without comment. Derrek had always been the quiet one, the dependable go-to-guy. Brent wouldn't be surprised if his best friend had a clock shoved up his ass; the man had never been late for anything. Reliable as the sun and almost as predictable was why Brent loved him—Derrek was everything Brent was not.

"Well, like my daddy said," Derrek motioned to the perky waitress in a low-cut black tee-shirt and a push-up bra that he was fairly certain was responsible for more of her tips than her service. "Better to keep your mouth shut and look stupid than open it and remove all doubt."

Brent turned his attention away from the plump backside of the young waitress and rolled his eyes. "That was Mark Twain, bro, not your daddy."

Derrek smirked underneath the shadow of his Stetson as if Brent crediting the quote wasn't impressive at all. "That's right, I forgot. You were the smart one in high school, getting into honors literature and all that crap. And looky here where all that book reading got you." He raised his bottle toward Brent. "Sitting right here next to me, drinking cheap beer, and checking out girls in push-up bras"

Brent laughed. It had been Derrek who'd received an offer for a full ride to the University of Texas. He'd turned it down after his parents' death in a boating accident ten years ago to run the family ranch and take care of his baby sister.

Brent still struggled with guilt for not being there for his friend during that dark time. Not wanting to bring up the painful past, he brought the conversation around to what was really important.

"So, do you know of any hot girls new to town? Anyone recently heartbroken and looking for a rebound?" Brent glanced around the crowded bar, checking out potential targets.

Instead of potential hook-ups, he noticed the the Sloan twins, Chandler and Tatum, slumming it at Everyday Joe's. Both were tall, dark, and handsome, if one took the "come-hither" looks all the ladies were tossing their way seriously. Maybe it had to do with their father's money, or that the powerful family had their fingers in just about every business around town. Either way, the Sloans were at the top of the list for most "eligible bachelor" in Somewhere.

Brent did a head nod toward the Sloans. "So, what's the story with them? Do they still own half the state and as rich as gods?"

Derrek shook his head. "You haven't heard? Sorry man, forgot to tell you. Sloan Sr. has cancer, and not the good kind."

Brent put down his beer. "Is there a good kind?"

"Well, if there is, it's not this one. I guess Dixie, the younger sister, and the mom are taking it hard."

Brent sighed. He remembered Dixie, a fresh-faced youth who always flashed her gap-toothed smile. She'd been younger than Brent and they hadn't run in the same crowd, but she'd always been pleasant to him when they saw each other around town. "How about Chandler and Tatum? They seem to be hanging in there."

"You know Tatum. Nothing affects him. He's still strumming on his guitar and driving motorcycles around town. Has no interest in taking over the family ranching business. Leaves all of it to Chandler."

Back in high-school, Brent and the twins used to hang out. At one point they formed a garage band that went nowhere, but when Brent moved away, he'd lost track of everyone. Now, seeing how much he'd missed, he felt guilty. "And Chandler?"

His friend's brow arched in a way that spoke way more than Derrek ever would. "You remember Chandler and his dad never saw eye to eye."

Brent nodded. "That's an understatement." He recalled some big rows between the two men. Even in this town they were legendary.

"But even before his dad got sick," Derrek continued, "Chandler changed. He's not the same cool guy we knew in high school."

"How so?"

"Now, he's a total dick."

Brent laughed. If Derrek said that about Chandler, it must be true. "Wasn't there another girl? The one who always hung out with the Sloans? She was kinda plain looking, really quiet. Like she was their sister or something, but wasn't?"

"Jayne," Derrek said.

Brent snapped his fingers. "Yeah. What about her?"

Derrek shrugged. "No one knows, man. The story is, one day she just up and left. No good bye, no nothing. No one's heard from her since."

Brent did a low whistle. "Yeah, and I thought I had issues."

"Right." Derrek nodded. "We've got nothing on the Sloans."

Brent let his gaze quickly move on, not wanting to waste his energy on things he couldn't change. He had more interesting things to do—women. "Anyway, hot girls? Rebound sex? Know of anyone who'd want to live out their fantasy of dating a rock star?"

"Don't make me pull out the video of you throwing up on stage and were caught lip-syncing." Derrek said, already picking up his phone.

Brent groaned and shook his head. "No, I was legitimately ill, and my agent assured me it's been pulled down."

"Oh no, I saved that mess on my phone. I'm going to be playing that video at your wedding," Derrek laughed.

He had no doubt his friend would do just that. Derrek got his twisted sense of humor and knew half of what Brent said was just hype. He also had no issue using it to cut him down a peg or two. "Remind me not to invite you," Brent mumbled into his beer.

"Sure thing, but seriously I don't know of anyone," Derrek said, finally getting back to Brent's previous question. "But if anyone could convince a girl to hook up for only one week it would be you. Just remember, my sister is at the ranch, and I'm sure she wouldn't appreciate feeding someone new each morning. Just keep it to the bunkhouse so I don't have to hear about it."

Brent was glad his low groan was covered up by the sound check from the three-piece band that had walked up on stage. He would've liked to say that he'd forgotten all about Danielle—Derrek's little sister—but that wasn't necessarily true. Danielle was just one of those people that didn't quite fit in his life. There was something about her that made him feel... uncomfortable?

Maybe...oh God...was it guilt?

The feelings he had toward Danielle were mixed. There were those feelings of a teenager who held down the pesky little sister of his best friend while Derrek waved his dirty socks in her face, and then there were those feelings of later —of noticing those pretty red lips, big, doe brown eyes, a contagious laugh, and the mouth that tasted of apple pie and summer.

He shook his head, disgusted with himself that his memory of her was so vivid. He hadn't seen her in close to ten years. Funny how he'd never asked Derrek if Danielle was dating anyone seriously. Maybe he hadn't wanted to know. "So what did Danielle say when you told her I was staying with you for a whole week?"

Derrek suddenly had a hard time holding Brent's gaze. "Umm... I didn't. I told her it was just a weekend. Been real busy on the ranch and didn't get around to letting her know. But she'll be cool. She shouldn't have an issue with it."

Brent hoped not. What had happened between them was ancient history. Child's play, really. If Danielle didn't have a problem with that kiss years ago, then Brent shouldn't either. He'd just have to remember to stay out of her way. The ranch was plenty big for both of them.

He planned to spend most of his time hunkered down in

the bunkhouse, finishing his album. Brent pushed the thought of her out of his mind. If he hadn't worked out his feelings about her in the last nine years, then he sure the hell wasn't going to figure them out in the next five minutes.

Derrek carefully wiped the condensation off the table with the drink napkin provided and stood. "I'll be right back, need to take the lizard for a walk. And I swear to God, if you ever see our waitress again, tackle her to get another round, will ya?"

Brent gave a mock salute and nodded. Spending time with his best friend felt good. Over the last few years they'd grown a bit distant. No one's fault, really, just too much time and too many miles between them. He hoped to rectify that.

TWO

*B*rent stretched out on the bench so he could face the main entrance and the dance floor. He loved watching people dance. Even after all these years, his favorite venues were the ones that had an open space for people to do the two-step or line dance.

The dance floor was fairly deserted, but of course the night was still young. The band that played was new, a group he hadn't heard of before. They called themselves Sugar Rush and had one jean-clad man on lead guitar, one on the drums, and a fairly hot girl in a slinky dress manning the mike. They were a cover band, no material of their own, but the girl's voice was pretty, and their range of songs was wide enough that the audience wouldn't get bored.

There were a few tables set up close to the stage, but they were pushed back from the actual dancing. A couple cowboys and their wives occupied the tables. Waitresses weaved in and out with trays full of beers and red plastic baskets of fried food.

When the band took five, Brent signaled to the young waitress again, but when she just nodded that she'd be there in a moment, he was pretty sure he'd die of thirst before he'd get a drink. Apparently, his fame could get him a comped suite in one of L.A's finest hotels, but not a beer order in Joe's two-bit bar.

His mood didn't improve any as the waitress stop at the Sloan table and Tatum began chatting her up. Brent rolled his eyes. Just get her number already and let the poor girl get on with her job.

Lord, he might have to actually get up and get his own drinks.

The front door opened, and the waning light from the setting sun spilled across the dusty floor. A few seconds later a woman in roughed up work boots and tight-fitting Wranglers strode in. Her back was partially toward him. With her hands on her hips and her neck craning as she searched the tables along the dance floor. Her boots were caked with mud, and her jeans were covered in dusty hand prints where she'd wiped the day's work away. Her tank top showed evidence of the Texas heat, even in early June, with the vee-shaped neckline and underarms dark from perspiration. Her profile was chiseled, and even from a distance he could tell that her strong jawline was offset by a feminine, messy ponytail underneath a brown Stetson that had seen better days.

The woman wasn't pretty in the classical way, or even in a fun, flirty way, but for some reason he couldn't take his eyes off her. She had a petite build with curves in all the right places. Her arms were sun-kissed and well-toned. Unlike some of the other women who were dressed to catch a man and more than likely hadn't been on a horse since they were kids, this woman all but screamed "Genuine Cowgirl."

She must've found what she was looking for, because

she bee-lined it for a portly man sitting near the front of the stage with two other men on either side of him. She walked up and slapped her palm flat on the table, her face low and close to the older man.

"Who the hell do you think you are, selling me cheap feed?"

She must've hit the table pretty hard, because his beer bottle wobbled, gave up the fight for balance, and spilled onto the man's lap.

The portly man jumped out of his chair with more speed than Brent would've given him credit for. "What the hell, DJ? You gonna pay for that beer?"

Brent recognized the gentleman now. He was old man Skinner, who owned the tack and feed store in town. Even when Brent had been a young kid, he'd never seen eye to eye with the crotchety old man. Skinner had always chased Brent and his friends out of the store when they took too long reading the comics. "If you're gonna read them, then you best be buying them!" he would shout out from behind the counter.

"You'd better be happy all you're getting is beer in your lap." The cowgirl's voice brought Brent back to the present as he took in the crowd's growing attention. "'Cause I've a mind to hit you square upside the head. You ever sell me that rye grass feed and charge me for alfalfa again, I'll come after you with a baseball bat, I swear to God."

Acknowledging the quieting audience, Skinner did his best to play his part. He shook his head, his eyes wide with surprise in his red face. "Jesus, DJ. I didn't know there was rye in it, I swear. I wouldn't do that to you."

That didn't seem to calm down the DJ chick any. In fact, Brent could almost see her vibrating with anger from where he was sitting. Personally, he hoped she did smack old man

Skinner upside the head. He knew he'd wanted to himself more than once.

"That's not what your clerk told me," she said, not backing down at all. "He told me you knew the feed had rye in it, but it was cheaper for you and you still charged me premium price. I've told you my horse is highly allergic to rye, and now he's been eating that crap for two days. The vet says his open sores and skin rash are due to a systemic allergic reaction. If my horse suffers any permanent damage because of your cheap ass, I'll be holding you personally responsible. So you better hope Majestic recovers, or I'll be coming after you."

"You'd better close that mouth of yours or people are going to start to think you're simple," Derrek said from behind Brent, a touch of humor underlying the words.

Brent startled. Maybe hanging half out of the booth so he could get a better view of one of the sexiest women he'd ever seen was a bit too obvious. Sure, he'd dated super models, but he knew this cowgirl could run circles around them. One thing Brent had learned in the music industry was that there was nothing more attractive than competence. "I think I've just found my next girl," he said, not even turning around to acknowledge his friend.

"Really?" Derrek's voice seemed amused.

Brent had no idea why. He hadn't been this serious about a girl since the last time he'd fallen in love. Which had been...well over three weeks ago. Ages.

With that conversation-stopper delivered, the woman turned around, which was a shame. Brent sure enjoyed eying that hot, little temper perfectly encased in a tight pair of jeans. But when she faced him, Brent wasn't disappointed —the front was even better than the back. Curvy frame, full breasts, high cheekbones, warm brown eyes.

He sighed. His interest was throughly captivated by a woman with a masculine name, a smart mouth, and a pretty face that grew more appealing by the minute.

Just then she caught sight of Derrek and started to walk over, but stopped and turned around. "Skinner, not only will I be expecting a full refund, I'm sending you the vet bill."

Skinner glared at her, but she'd already turned and was walking away.

Derrek groaned. "God, that temper of hers is going to get her in big trouble one of these days."

"You know her?" Brent asked, getting the familiar flutters in his stomach, watching her hips sway as she closed the distance between them. What was it about a woman that knew what she wanted and wasn't afraid to get it that he found so enticing?

Derrek coughed. "Ahh, yes... a little."

What was wrong with his friend? Was he already clamming up at the thought of talking to a pretty woman? Derrek had the habit of undercutting Brent's cool by pulling some old-world crap like standing up and pulling out a lady's chair, or opening car doors for them. As much as women said they liked that kinda stuff, the gentleman always seemed to find himself alone, while the bad boy whistled all the way to a home run.

Without losing sight of his target, Brent threw out a few words to his friend, coaching him, before she was within earshot. "Don't do anything stupid, Derrek. Keep your mouth shut and let me handle this. Her name's DJ, right?"

"Um... yeah, DJ." He coughed again. "And if you think you can handle her..."

The rest was left unsaid, but Brent wasn't scared. There was nothing he liked better than a challenge.

DJ got to their booth, where she tossed her hat on to the

table and blew some stray strands of black hair off her face. Her strong features may put off some people, but Brent was of a different mind. While her sharp cheekbones and strong chin could've cut ice, her eyes were enough to set a man on fire.

The only truly soft and completely feminine thing about her was her mouth. Full, naturally pink lips that hinted at a wide smile and possibly an opened-mouth laugh. To see those lips turn and tip upward instead of pressed into a thin line was a task he was more than up for.

She reached over and grabbed Derrek's beer and took a long swig, finishing the drink off. Brent found he couldn't look away from how the long column of her throat worked and the rise and fall of her chest between each breath.

"Ever hear that you'll catch more flies with honey than vinegar?" Derrek said.

She plopped the bottle down. "Says you."

"Says just about everyone."

The butterfly wings that seconds before danced merrily, dried to dust in his mouth. This DJ seemed way too comfortable with Derrek. Could he have a claim on her? He studied Derrek's face, who looked more annoyed than infatuated.

DJ's dark eyes ponged upward. "Then these 'everyones' have never dealt with the likes of Skinner McDavid."

For the first time, DJ looked his way. Brent sat up straighter and tried for his not-so-eager smile.

"What the hell's wrong with him?" DJ asked with a nod in Brent's direction.

Derrek shrugged. "He's found his next vict... um, girlfriend."

The crease between DJ's eyes deepened. There was

nothing Brent wanted to do more than to kiss it away. "Who?"

"You." Derrek said.

There was a bark of laugher that sounded sharp and not at all humorous. "Does he know who—"

"Please, please don't ruin this." Derrek cut her off.

Brent didn't like how this conversation was going and finally decided to take control. "It looks like you're thirsty. Can I buy you a drink?" He didn't wait for her answer, just rushed in before she had time to use her better judgment. "Let me guess, Appletini with a twist?"

Women loved when he tried to guess their drink. Made him look perceptive and that he cared. Usually he nailed it right off.

She just looked at him like he had two heads. Maybe she'd never been wooed by the likes of him before. Not many could put on the charm like he could. She shook her head. "No, I need to get up early in the morning. I was just about to head off."

"You're leaving?" He meant for that to come out less astonished than it sounded, but he really was surprised. "You're upset because I guessed the wrong drink? Give me another shot, please." He added his best smile to seal the deal. "You're a regular old beer gal. I think girls who drink beer are sexy."

She put both her arms on the table and rested her chin in her hands. "Wait, are you really trying to pick me up?"

He got closer, covering half the distance between them while his heart rate kicked up to the next level. This was what he loved. He never felt more alive than when he was chasing his muse. "And are you really trying to play hard to get?"

Her face changed from disbelief to pure astonishment.

"Oh, I'm playing, alright, and I don't think I've ever enjoyed myself so much. So let me ask you."

She leaned in real close. Close enough that if Brent wanted to, he could kiss her. Was that what she wanted? He let his gaze fall to her mouth—damn, she had beautiful lips. She must have seen him staring, because she chose just that moment to lick them.

Easy boy. "Ask away, Sugar. To you, I'm an open book," he said.

There was a mischievous twinkle in her eyes that was right up Brent's alley. How did she know he loved mischievous? "Does that 'let-me-guess-your-drink' line ever work?"

All the time.

"I wouldn't know. You're the first I ever wanted to ask," his voice the low, sexy rumble that he'd perfected when he sang his love songs.

"Wow, does it bother your conscience to lie that easily?" Her tone sweet, with the airiness of cotton candy, but without the stomachache afterwards.

"I'd never lie to you, Sugar."

"Somehow, I don't believe that." The girl was quick, he'd give her that. It was taking everything he had to keep one step ahead of her.

"Believe this." He took her hand and brought her ring finger up to his mouth and kissed it. "I see you don't have a ring. Can I assume you're unattached?"

She didn't pull away. He took that as a yes.

"And neither am I. What a wonderful coincidence, don't you think?"

She shook her head, her mouth slightly parted. "I'm speechless."

"Here then, let me help." He took her hand and flipped it palm up. Then took out the pen he kept around just for this reason. He carefully wrote his full name and number down.

She stared at the digits.

"Recognize the name?" he asked. This was his favorite part.

"Brent Kane. Should I?" He didn't quite trust the sincerity in her voice, but he was nothing if not reckless.

"Ever hear of the songs, Girl, I Love You or It's Been A Long Time?"

She nodded, her face giving nothing away.

"Those are my songs."

Wait for it.

"Oh." Her hand came up to her chest.

Here it comes.

"Oh," the word floated out of her mouth with an unseen exclamation point rising up from behind. "So you're that country singer?"

He did that one sided smile that made his dimple show. "I prefer rock star, but yes, ma'am, I am."

She pulled her hand away to examine the numbers more closely. "So this here's a rock star's phone number on my hand? I have the chance to be a booty-call for a living, breathing celebrity?"

Well, those wouldn't be the terms he would use, but women seemed more understanding of men these days. He touched the brim of his hat. "I'm here for a whole week."

Her smile grew wide and her eyes narrowed dangerously as she spit in her hand, wiped her palm on his shirt sleeve, and then got up and walked away.

Brent gaped as she sashayed away from his booth and out of his life.

"Damn," Derrek slapped his hand on the table. "I've never seen anything quite like that before."

Neither had Brent. "I know."

"Oh, bro," Derrek said. "That girl just spit in her own hand to wipe your number off."

Brent was at a total loss. He couldn't remember the last time a woman turned him down. "I know. I think I'm in love."

THREE

*D*J wiped her palm off on her jeans once, then twice for good measure, as she weaved her way between the parked cars on the lot, the night air doing nothing to cool her temper. *Yuck.* The whole thing grossed her out and pissed her off at the same time. Who did Brent think he was? Obviously, some type of God's gift to women. DJ rolled her eyes. Brent had always been too conceited for his own good. Must come with the package of having those all-American good looks and too many women willing to fall for them. Even when she'd been a kid and he'd been just a teenager with nothing more than a few guitar chords under his belt, she remembered him telling her he was going to be a star one day. Even back then she'd known he was full of himself. Of course, he did go on to be one of country music's biggest stars, and she believed that his first album went platinum. Not that she kept track or anything.

DJ smashed her hat on to her head and jumped in the old, mint-green Ford pickup truck. In a town of big trucks and fancy chrome wheels, her ride was a total throwback, and she... hated it. There were lots of things left over from her parents, the house, the ranch, the debts, and, last but not least, the damn truck.

Derrek had always been funny about not wanting to let certain things of their parents' go. For some reason he had attached sentimental value to this ugly green machine, but then again, he wasn't the one who had to drive it. She didn't know what it was with men and old trucks, but if given a choice, she'd have picked shiny and new any day. She had a ranch to run, horses to pull, loads to haul. It was real hard getting the job done when her only mode of transportation was a throwback to the days of her grandfather. Sure, she could've put her foot down and said she wanted a new truck, but since there wasn't money in the budget for an actual truck payment, she'd rather let her brother think she was as sentimental as he.

She turned the ignition and took her frustration out by grinding through the truck's manual gears. The whole day had gone to hell in a hand basket, from waking up to a sick horse, to a ranch-hand getting hurt because he wasn't paying attention, to the vet's diagnosis—allergic reaction from bad hay. She'd gone into a panic. How come no one had caught that the feed order was wrong? It had taken her and her men the rest of the morning to change the feed and administer treatments to get Derrek's horse, Majestic, comfortable. She just prayed he would recover and not have any lingering issues. She couldn't afford another vet bill. The ranch was cutting it close each month as it was; she sure as hell couldn't make it with her best stud down.

DJ shook her head. And then there was Brent. Anger and hurt had her pressing the gas pedal to the floor as she tried to get the old clunker up to speed. She looked down at the black smear of ink on her palm. Really, after all these years, *this* was their first communication?

How many years had it taken her to keep from jumping up every time the phone rang just in case it was him? How many times had she scrolled through her brother's cell to see if anywhere in Brent's text he had mentioned her? Too many times to count, and way too many to admit to and still have a little self-respect.

But really, treating her as a *booty call*? That was a new low even for Brent Kane. True, it had been close to ten years since they'd seen each other, but Brent should've known he wouldn't get anywhere with her. She'd foolishly been taken in before, but at twenty-four and already feeling twice that, she was far from the naive young thing of their youth.

She shook her wrist to dislodge the tingling sensation that lingered from when he held her hand. There might've been a time in her life—grieving and foolishly infatuated—when she would've considered being Brent's one-night-stand. Of course, not even under threat of torture would she admit that. Now, she had more pressing things in her life than a pair of long legs and a sexy-blue eyed gaze.

The ranch was in the black, but just barely, and now it wasn't just her and Derrick whose livelihood depended on it. It was also the ranch hands and seasonal workers who had families and other responsibilities. There was a whole lot riding on keeping things afloat, and there were times, more often than not, that those worries kept her up at night. The last thing she needed was Brent to waltz in and create more work for her with his entitlement issues. No, the sooner he was back to his highfalutin lifestyle, the better.

Only one weekend. One weekend, that's what Derrek had told her. Except, Brent had said one week. She must've misheard. She didn't even know if she could put up with Brent for that long. Too bad she'd never been one to resist taking a haughty man down a few pegs. It was one of her flaws, really. That and her temper—according to Derrek. She rolled her eyes.

I'm a rock star.

She almost gagged. Like that was any kind of endorsement. She would bet he'd slept with over half the women under the age of twenty-five who'd been impressed by that title. The man was a dog; she just had to make sure she didn't catch his fleas.

Brent stumbled as he made his way out of the bunkhouse and into the sunshine. Damn, was the sun brighter here than in L.A.? Either way, he needed some coffee in order to make it through. He dragged himself past the stables and up the few steps that led to the back door.

The door opened up into a sunny kitchen that was already heavy with the aromas of breakfast—eggs and toast, by his guess. The kitchen had a well-used, cluttered look that was mostly due to a large rectangular table surrounded by high-back wooden chairs. Derrek was seated at one end, hunched over a newspaper and a cup of coffee—a plate full of eggs off to the side.

"Good morning," Brent said, already eying his friend's full plate of food. He usually didn't have a big breakfast when he woke up. Most of the time he either ate on the run or just started his day with lunch.

Derrek looked up, gave him a stiff once over, and winced. "Hard night?"

Brent raked his hands through his hair. Had it been? He was a little hung over, though he didn't think he'd drunk all that much, but something must've gone wrong, since he'd woken up without a cute backside warming his bed. That was probably why he didn't feel like writing this morning. His muse had slipped through his fingers. Brent pulled out a chair, the wooden back creaking as he slumped into it, a bit grumpy. It was still morning, after all. "I must be losing my touch, since I totally got smacked down by that hot piece of tail last night. I don't know what her issue was, but a woman that uptight could only mean she needs to get laid. And I mean... *bad*. She'd be in a lot better mood this morning if she'd accepted my offer last night."

Derrek's eyebrows shot up, and his wide-eyed gaze darted behind Brent and then back again.

Brent knew that look. He sighed, turned his head around and took in the woman with her back toward him, cooking on the stove. He grimaced. Really, that hadn't been a conversation meant for anyone else's ears. Total guy talk and not appropriate for ladies, and from the look of how she filled out those jeans, she was *all* woman.

His mama had taught him better, and to be shooting his mouth off as a guest in someone else's home—he shook his head—he'd been in L.A. too long. "Sorry, ma'am, not really appropriate talk over the breakfast table."

She turned around and shot him a gaze from the same warm dark eyes and wide mouth he remembered from the bar last night.

"Certainly, Brent." She walked over and placed a plate of food in front of him. Her lips were as inviting as a barbed-wire fence, while her eyes held enough disdain that he could almost choke on it. "I've been called a pain in the ass, but never a hot piece of tail this early in the morning. Coffee's in the pot. Help yourself."

Brent stared down at his plate and tried to piece things together. What the hell? Had he been wrong about Derrek and DJ last night? Had he just made a play on his best friend's girl? And he was a guest in this man's house. How much of a dick was he?

"You could've just told me she was with you," Brent said, pushing his eggs around with his fork. "I wouldn't have tried to pick her up if I had known." Why did his voice sound all stiff and angry? *He* was the one who'd just called his friend's chick a hot piece of ass. And yet, there was a green-eyed monster who wanted to come out and rear its ugly head. Was he really jealous of his friend's girl?

Brent needed to double check. He turned around and took in her slim-fitting Wranglers, tight tank top that emphasized her high breasts, and tan, fit shoulders. Her hair was up in a messy ponytail and her face free of any make-up, but hell yeah, he was jealous. He turned around to glare at his best friend

Derrek choked on his coffee.

"Ahh, yeah, buddy, choking is a potential risk when you try to laugh and drink at the same time," Brent said, feeling less and less amused by the moment.

Derrek worked the coffee down and wiped at his eyes. Brent doubted they were tears of sadness. "Brent, you really don't recognize who she is? This is Danielle. You know my sister, Danielle? The one we used to torture and call 'The Brat.'"

Two things happened at once. First, Brent felt like the world's biggest idiot, and second, relief flooded through him at the realization that this woman didn't belong to Derrek in that way.

DJ sat down opposite of her brother with a large cup of coffee in her hands. "Oh man," she said, her voice a bit too cheery on a hang-over morning. "You should see your face right now. You look about as surprised as one of those men getting a positive paternity test on a daytime talk show."

Brent shook his head. "No, no, old man Skinner called you DJ. If he would've said Danielle I'd have put two and two together."

She snorted, as if doubting his ability to do simple math. "I started going by my initials years ago—Danielle Jessica. Brent's the only one who still calls me Danielle."

Brent looked from one sibling's self-satisfied smirk to the other and groaned. "You both knew what I was doing and you let me." He turned to Derrek. "You're supposed to be my best friend, which means you stop me from making a fool out of myself."

Derrek rested his elbow on the table, his shoulders shaking with silent laughter. "Bro, it was just too priceless. I'd thought you'd figure it out soon enough, but before I knew it you already were spewing your overworked lines and celebrity status. And I don't mind saying that it felt good to see you get turned down for once, even if it was by my own sister."

"Oh my goodness," DJ piped in, like knocking him down a few pegs was turning out to be the best part of her day. "My favorite line out of the whole thing was 'I prefer rock star, but yes, ma'am, I am.'" She fanned her hand in front of her face. "I can't believe you've actually gotten a bite off that tired line."

Um, yeah, it worked. He usually only had to say "rock st—" before some woman went home with him. Others just dropped to their knees. He preferred both, of course. "Yes, but when *I* say rock star, I make it sound so much better."

She laughed, stood to refill her coffee and then brought him a cup of his own. "So I believe Derrek told me that I only have to put up with you for one more day. You're just here through Sunday, right?"

Brent took a sip of coffee and shook his head. "No, I told Derrek I was going to be here all week."

"All week?"

Now it was his turn to smirk. Apparently, she hadn't been informed. "Oh yeah, *all* week."

She looked from him to Derrek—who seemed overly concerned with a hearing aid advertisement—and back again.

DJ propped a hand on her hip and gave him an unhindered view of her sharpened cheekbones. "So, what's your plan for the week?"

He'd almost forgotten why he loved hanging out at Derrek's house—getting under DJ's skin was as easy and satisfying as a cool swim on a hot day. Brent may be pushing thirty, but it didn't mean he'd grown up any.

He took his time scooping the eggs onto toast, then closed his eyes and savored each bite as if he were dining at a five star restaurant. He could feel her bristle across from him. Patience had never been DJ's strong suit. "The usual," he said. "Just relax. Sleep in. Not have to be anywhere at any time. Enjoy being in the same bed for a week. I'm sure I can find someone willing to share it with me."

He threw in the last line out of spite. Maybe he wasn't quite over the way she'd teased him last night.

"Right," she nodded stiffly. "So, in other words, do what you've always done. Nothing."

His smile tightened like the cinching up on a horse's saddle. His whole issue with DJ came flying back. Even as a kid she'd never believed in him. He'd gotten way too much of that from his parents, so when his friend's little sister had started insinuating that his music was just a pipe dream, he'd taken offense. But she'd been that way with so many things. Ever since he could remember she had tattled on them. She'd turned her nose up at whatever cool idea or fun thing they had wanted to try, and she'd always gotten in the way of their picking up girls.

"Ever hear of the term "kill joy?'" he asked.

Her teeth ground edge on edge as the two-handed grip on her coffee cup rivaled one on the Demon Death Drop ride at the amusement park. "Don't start, Brent. I'm not in the mood."

"It's called having fun." He talked over her between bites of toast and eggs. "It might help with that 'up-tightness' that was mentioned before."

He watched her jaw work behind her lush lips before she finally forced out a loud ha. "Well, having 'fun'," she emphasized with air quotes, "might be for those who don't have a ranch to run. You know, for the rest of us who have to actually work."

Okay, now it was on. Irritated, he put his fork down and turned to follow her with his gaze as she made her way back to the stove. Teasing DJ was only fun when he didn't get provoked back. "Well, if being on a world-tour for the last two years is lazy, I'd hate to see your idea of work."

DJ set her cup in the sink, then folded her hands and tilted her head up in pious mockery. "Oh, please God, when I die let me come back as a pretty boy with a passable voice so all I'll have to do is strum a few chords on my guitar and gyrate my hips in order to make a living."

He got to his feet. Why the hell had he thought he'd found his muse last night? More like his Achilles' heel. "If that's what you think—"

"That's enough, you two," Derrek cut him off. "I want to read my paper in peace and not hear you two bicker like an old married couple. Brent, stay out of DJ's way. She has a real busy couple of weeks. And DJ," he looked at her and shook his head. "Go... go see to the horses. Since you cooked, we'll do the dishes."

DJ shrugged and grabbed a thermos off the counter, but stopped before she headed out the back door. "Oh, Brent, by the way," her eyes snapping like black twinkle lights, her lips tight in a pretend smile, "a late breakfast is only served on Sundays. If you want to eat in the mornings we start our day at six a.m. sharp. This isn't a bed and breakfast, and no matter how inflated your ego, we don't cater to rock stars here."

He mirrored her smirk perfectly as he raised his coffee cup in a mock salute. "I'll be fine with coffee, thank you very much, but your hospitality is outstanding."

Her answer—the unsatisfying slamming of the door behind her. He slumped back into his chair and pushed his plate away. How did she know just the right thing to say to irritate him?

"You're right, you know."

Brent looked up, but his friend's roughened face and serious eyes were still buried behind the paper. Brent had been right? How so? Trying to get the world's most uptight woman into his bed or goading the hand that was literally feeding him? "About what?"

Brent waited as Derrek finished his breakfast and folded the newspaper off to the side. His best friend had his own pace about him, and Brent knew from past experience that nothing could rush him.

"About her needing to have more fun," Derrek said. "Working all the time is fine for me. I've been an old man since I was eighteen, but she's still young. She shouldn't spend all her time at the ranch. This place can take your years and your soul, and if there's one thing I've learned from my parents' death, it is the need to enjoy life more. I've been pushing her to find friends her own age, go shopping with some girlfriends, anything, but none of those things interest her. So that's why when you called, I thought it couldn't have been better. I'm hoping you can help me out."

Brent looked up. Him help Derrek? All their lives it had been the other way around. Derrek had been the one to bail Brent out of more trouble than a teenage boy should get into. He'd probably saved his life more than once by talking Brent into a more prudent course. If there was any way he could help his friend out, Brent was all for it. "Sure, you know I'd lay down my life for you."

Derrek laughed. "Ah, Brent, that's what I've always loved about you. You're always so extreme. From one end to the other and no in-between." He shook his head. "No, nothing that serious. I just want DJ to have some fun. Looking back, you were the one person who seemed to enjoy life to the fullest. Every minute was a party, every day something to look forward to, so if anyone could get Danielle to loosen up and live a little, it'd be you."

Brent made a show of glancing around the room. Was Derrek serious? Had he even been in the same room when DJ and he were speaking? "She hates my guts."

"She hates everyone's guts. It's like..." He circled his hand as he waited for the right word to come to him. "...like you're a womanizer. She's a hater. It's just her thing. You can't take it personally."

Great. No, he wouldn't take it personally. He just had to take time away from his music to help the world's most uptight person learn to have fun. "Let me get this right. Do you want me to take your sister out? Like on a date?"

"You didn't seem to have a problem with it last night." Derrek's tone mimicked the dry rustling of the newspaper he was reading.

"That was before I knew she was your sister. That *she* was Danielle." He was pretty sure his muse wouldn't be hiding in a platonic relationship.

"Well, now that you do know," Derrek said, getting up and patting him on the back, "you can make sure to treat her with respect. Don't look so worried, bro, it's not like Danielle is going to want to sleep with you or anything. She's got better sense than that."

"And why am I such a bad guy?" Had he really asked that? It almost seemed like he cared what DJ thought of him —which he didn't.

"You know," Derrek said, gave him a once over, and gestured to his hair. "The scruffy hair, the unkempt, ruffled look, like you just rolled out of bed."

"Ahh…,because I just did." Did he sound defensive? Well, he wasn't.

Derrek shrugged as if the truth of the matter was of little consequence. "Yeah, she still doesn't go for those types."

"And by type, you mean a rock star? Because dude, every girl goes for a rock star." Yeah, a total douche-bag line, but it got a smile out of Derrek.

"Not DJ, but I encourage you to use that line again and see if it gets you any further," Derrek said as he threw the blue dish towel in Brent's face. He did a quick survey of the kitchen. "You good with the dishes?"

Brent shook his head. "Um… I haven't cleaned a kitchen in like five years."

Derrek nodded, "In that case, don't use the steel wool on the pans and remember to take out the garbage. Appreciate it, bro."…and followed his sister out the door.

FOUR

*B*rent cracked an eyelid, then quickly buried his head in his pillow and groaned. He wasn't in his own bed. He was intimate with that feeling, but had never been comfortable with it. When he'd been younger and just starting out, he'd spent a lot of time in cheap hotels and on other people's couches, but neither of those had happened in a while. Now, he traveled the U.S. in a custom tour trailer with a king size bed and a big screen TV in the back.

He groaned and stretched his lower back. He had outfitted his trailer with a special orthopedic bed that contoured to his body when he slept. This mattress, however, was thinner than an anorexic meth-head, and the sheets were as over-used and under-washed as those at a charge-by-the-hour motel. He may just have to outfit himself with a new bed for the duration of his stay here.

He looked around at the sparse, open-style bunk house. It had been updated a bit since he and Derrek used to crash here when they were younger. At first, the bunkhouse had been used for video game marathons and junk food sprees, but as they'd gotten older it became a place to bring girls home and practice his music.

Music. Funny how just being here brought back so many memories. He'd had high hopes when he'd called Derrek to ask him if he could crash here. Sure, he could've put himself up in any one of the fancier hotels in town, or even stayed with his parents, who were still in the very same house in which he'd grown up, right here in Somewhere. Hell, he could've booked a nice trip to Barbados and written songs in a hammock while sipping an umbrella drink. But none of those options would get him closer to what he hoped to find —his muse.

He'd had such passion, such drive, when he'd been younger. All he'd ever wanted to do was eat, drink, and sleep music. He'd wanted to share his passion, tell his story through his guitar so badly, that he'd thought he'd go up in flames with the need of it. In hindsight, it was more than likely sexual frustration of an average adolescent boy than star lust, but no one could've told him that back then. Other than girls, which ran a close second, writing songs was all he'd thought about. He would go to school all day, work in the evening, and then come home and still have the energy to write music. Sometimes till two a.m., and then wake up and do it all over again.

The terms "burn-out" and "writer's block" meant nothing to him then. He'd been young, energetic, and damn near invincible. Nothing could touch him. Music had poured out of him like sweat off a boxer in a ring. He'd think of whole songs while driving his truck from school to home. He'd come up with a chorus in the shower and the bridge while he downed some food.

Those days seemed like eons ago, not a mere decade.

Well, he needed some of that passion back fast. His manager had called again last night, but Brent didn't have to listen to the voice mail to know what Sally had said. Had he started writing yet? Did he have a new song? Did he understand that the recording studio was already booked?

Brent pushed himself to sitting and massaged his aching head. God, what he wouldn't give to have Teresa, his personal masseuse, here right now. But no, that was the whole point. He needed to get back to basics and find his spark again. When he'd first moved to Nashville, he'd thought the world ended and began along those paved streets and gold stars. The buzz of the city, the sheer excitement, had made him unable to sleep the first week he was there. It hadn't taken long to realize that aspiring artists were a dime a dozen and that picking up paying gigs was about as easy as convincing a clean pig to stay out of the mud. So when one of his songs actually made it to the charts, he'd thought he would never have to work again. Writing and singing songs wasn't work—it was his life. But now life seemed to be bogged down with one publicity event after the next, and work was anything that had to do with his guitar.

Brent glanced around and took in the other set of bunk beds adjacent to him and the large overstuffed leather couches that circled the big screen TV like covered wagons. The stained concrete floor chilled his bare feet, while the sun streaming from behind the closed mini-blinds was bright enough to coax even this cowboy from his bed before noon.

God, he hated country hours.

Well, here he was. He had the stillness, the quietness, of no commitments, no publicity dates, and no rock concerts.

There was nothing to fill his days except for a pencil, a spiral notebook, and his first Seagull acoustic guitar. Today was the day that he would write his next song. Today was the day of no distractions, no phone, no Internet, no... freaking stimulus.

Yep.

No distractions.

Just him.

Just him and these four walls.

God, he needed some coffee.

He quickly threw back the covers, pulled on a pair of jeans and a shirt, and slipped on his flip flops to make his way out to the main house. He just hoped he wasn't too late for some breakfast.

He hadn't quite made it up in time for breakfast, but miracle of miracles there was some coffee left. He poured some into a cup and watched the timer count down as he nuked it.

"Good morning, Rock Star. Wasn't sure if you were going to be sleeping the whole morning away."

It had taken Brent a whole thirty seconds to figure out that someone was calling him Rock Star, and that someone besides his mother was criticizing his sleeping patterns. He turned around, expecting to see a playful smile on DJ's lips, but instead saw a pursed mouth and one perfectly arched brow. She sat on the far side of the kitchen table with a bowl in front of her and an over-sized coffee cup. Maybe it was the smug look on her face, or maybe her overtly rude rejection of him the other night still stung, but either way, he couldn't resist poking the bear a bit. "Isn't that the pot calling the kettle black, since you're finishing breakfast a few minutes before I am?"

Her twilight eyes narrowed, and her tight-mouthed expression emphasized those razor-sharp cheek bones. When had she gotten so exotic looking? She'd always been just Danielle, but now she looked like a woman who had secrets that were begging to be exposed. He wondered what her midnight hair would look like spread out across his bed. She swept up her dishes in one efficient move and pushed past him toward the dishwasher. "This is what regular people call 'eating lunch.' It's the meal in between morning and evening. You know, halfway through the work day."

No longer wanting to torture himself, Brent turned around and fumbled in the refrigerator door, looking for the creamer. He knew he'd seen it somewhere yesterday, but for the life of him he couldn't remember where he'd put it. "Half way? I know you country folk like to keep early hours, but don't you think that's a little exaggeration?"

"Is this what you're looking for?" A blue bottle of French vanilla creamer was slammed down on the counter next to him. "Someone had to get up extra early to go to the store since you finished the creamer yesterday. And no, that wasn't an exaggeration. Up at four. Out in the stables by six. By the time you roll out of bed, more than half of my day is over."

He opened the creamer and splashed a little into his cup. Had he really finished off the creamer yesterday? The decent thing would've been to run to the store and pick up some for breakfast, but in reality he hadn't even thought about it. He rarely ever went to the store anymore. He had a full time assistant that took care of all the "house duties" when he was at home. Most of the time, he just left the empty container on the counter and, a new item would magically reappear in his refrigerator.

He leaned against the counter so he could look at her. He hadn't laid eyes on her for over ten years, and it seemed as if he was having a hard time getting his fill. "Are the horses even up at that hour? I mean, I do hope that you at least let them sleep in on Sundays – or do you work them as hard as you do everyone else around here?"

That got her skirt starched. He found he had a bad habit of liking to get under her skin. Too bad that wasn't the only thing he'd like to get under. The curse of years of easy women—his self-restraint was a little weak.

"My horses are well taken care of," she said. Her voice was tight as if needing to prove something. Interesting. To whom was she trying to prove herself? Certainly, not him.

"I didn't say that they weren't well taken care of. I said they were over worked like the rest of your employees." He watched as she gripped the counter in an effort, no doubt, to keep her hands from around his neck. He remembered the temper she'd displayed at Everyday Joe's, and knew he was playing with fire. But hell, someone around here needed to stand up to her. Derrek seemed to let her run the show most of the time by staying out of her way and taking care of the business side of things while he let her deal with the men and the horses.

"I don't expect anything more from my employees than what I do myself," she said, a finger pointing to her chest. "I'm the first one there and the last one to leave at night. There's nothing I would expect from my men that I don't do myself."

He crossed one flip-flop clad foot over the other. One of the first rules on the ranch was to have proper footwear, and he knew it annoyed the hell out of her that he was wearing shoes that were more conducive to the beach than to ranching. He saw her glance down, so he wiggled his toes a bit. In contrast, DJ had on work boots, already covered with a fine layer of dust, a pair of well-worn jeans, and another sleeveless tank that showed off those muscular arms of hers. He wondered if she owned anything other than tank-tops and jeans.

She braced her elbow against the counter and leaned back. If she knew how her stance made her breasts push against the fabric of her shirt, she'd be mortified. Good thing he knew how to keep a secret. "So, you think twelve hour days, six days a week, is a perfectly acceptable way to live?"

She tossed her head to flip long strands of black hair out of her face, he believed, the better to laser him with those dark eyes of hers. "My men know that they are allowed to leave when their shift is over at three."

"Right, and like any of them would be willing to leave before their boss does."

"That's their choice." She straightened to her full height of five-four. She was such a little thing. It was impressive that she ran this ranch like a well-oiled machine with no more than a raised eyebrow and a stern look. "They don't have to work here if they don't want to. I pay them well and treat them fairly."

Brent held up his hand. "Okay, fine. Let's forget about your men and your horses for one moment. Not sure if that is possible, but let's try. I'll give you another example... your brother."

That did it. If she was irritated before then she was pissed now. He'd never seen two siblings so protective of each other. "What about my brother?"

He remembered the weary look on his friend's face when he'd admitted to being an old man by age eighteen. Brent had always felt guilty about not being as good a friend as Derrek, so if Brent could make Derrek's life easier in some small way, he would. Even if that meant taking on his hell-cat of a sister. Brent took a sip of coffee to fortify himself. "He's tied to this ranch more than any prisoner on a chain gang. I'll bet my newest guitar that he hasn't had a day off in months. Your passion might be in taking care of the horses, but there's no way running this ranch since he was eighteen isn't taking a toll on him."

That might've hit too close to home. He watched her throat work hard to swallow and the look in her eyes bordered on hurt more than anger. He almost apologized, until he heard her next words. "Funny, what you've just described is what regular people do to earn a living. It's called 'work' for a reason. So, if you're done lecturing me on the way of the world per a playboy's point of view, I've got other things to do."

Okay, two could play at this game. Apparently, she wasn't the only person whose skin could get crawled under. If he knew her buttons then she knew his. His father was forever telling him to quit music and get a real job. One would think his dad would've stopped once Brent had a hit record, but no. "I work."

Her brow furrowed as she tilted her head. "Oh what? I'm sorry, are you working right now? Is *this* working? Is your slouching around my kitchen drinking your cup of coffee with my creamer working? Because if so, please let me know, and I'll come back when you're on a break. You know, when you're more relaxed with less... *work* on your mind." The word work was emphasized, complete with finger quotes and a pinning look that had him questioning picking a fight with her this early in the day.

"Do you know how competitive the country music business is?" he shot back. Now who sounded like they were trying to prove themselves?

"Oh, I'm sure. There are always tons of people out there that want to get paid for doing nothing." She took a few steps and braced her elbows on the counter closest to him. Her shirt gaped a bit, showing the smallest fringe of black lace bra underneath. Practical, no-nonsense, rough-around-the edges, DJ wore lacy underthings? What the hell? And black ones at that? That morsel of information was not going to help him sleep at night.

"Wow, that's pretty judgmental of you."

"Color me ashamed." She didn't look ashamed. In fact, she looked down right smug, and he, for one, was sick of fighting with her. More than anything, he wanted to shut her up. He remembered another time when he rendered her speechless—of how her mouth tasted as her lips opened, unsure and tentative. Of how her fingers gripped his shirt and her legs wrapped around his sides, causing him to just about lose his mind.

He looked at the self-righteous tilt of her mouth, the jut of her chin, and shook his head. He was a risk-taker by nature, and consequences were just something that came later, but were never important in the heat of the moment. He did what he always did. He saw. He wanted. He took.

Brent set his coffee down and closed the distance between them, pinning her into the corner with just his body. Without approval, without permission, he palmed her face and brought her mouth up to his.

Startled might've been a good word to describe DJ's reaction. Anger might've been a better one, but he'd wanted a taste of those lips since the night he'd seen her in the bar. So, if he was going to get hell for kissing her, than it damn well would be because he kissed her thoroughly and not because of some half-hearted attempt.

Her mouth opened under his, probably with the intention of biting, but he didn't give her a chance. His tongue swept alongside hers, and it took him a half a second to claim her mouth with his own. She softened slightly. He took her yield and pressed his advantage. A kiss that had started with the goal of simple peace and quiet had changed to anything but *simple* and his no longer giving a damn about *quiet*. Her body was flush against him. Her fingers fisted in his shirt.

And then she moaned.

He would've been fine. Been able to pull back and make some kind of witty remark, but that low whimper in the back of her throat that fired his desire and urgency all at the same time had him reacting.

He couldn't help himself. This was how he lived, full throttle or nothing at all. He filled his palms with the most delicious backside he ever remembered seeing and lifted her up onto the counter. Her legs found purchase around his waist and in no time at all he deepened the kiss. There could be no doubt what they were doing. This was a bedroom kiss, a prelude-to-sex kiss, a there's-no-way-in-hell-I'm -not-taking-you-up-against-the-wall-and-finishing-this kiss.

She pulled away first. It must've been her, because he was all about getting down to what they'd started ten years ago. He'd let her go then, but they weren't children any longer. No, she was a full grown woman, and if a full grown woman kissed a man like that then there damn well would be consequences.

He rested his hands on the counter on either side of her hips, his mind quickly calculating the chances of picking her up and carrying her to the bedroom before that bewildered, lust-haze expression was gone from her face. Her lips were parted and soft, breath fast and quick, and her fingers had found their way into the waistband of his pants.

They both looked down at her hand. She with shock on her face, and him with pure pleasure in his heart. "If I didn't know any better, I would say it looks as if you're trying to get into my pants."

She snatched her hand back, and before he could placate her with another kiss she was off the counter and across the kitchen.

He stifled a groan of disappointment. He just had to go and open his big, fat mouth.

She shoved her hair out of her face, and then got real busy straightening her shirt, as if working on a ranch required her to be wrinkle free. "So like I was saying." Her gaze darted everywhere but at him. "I need to get back to work."

He liked seeing her discombobulated. It did great things for his ego. "And I would like to get back to the work that we were just doing."

She threw her shoulders back and looked him square in the face as if she hadn't just had her tongue in his mouth a moment ago. "And now I see why you're having problems finishing your album. You're confusing work with play. I guess that's one of the drawbacks of being a rock star. It's gotta be hard to remember which is which. Well, if you're looking for inspiration for what real working men do during the day, you're always welcome to work your back on my ranch. There are always jobs that require more brute strength than smarts." She punctuated her dig with the turn of her heel and a view of her backside as she walked out the door.

He let her go with that comment, but only because he could barely hold back a laugh. He'd seen her face and knew how flustered she'd been. That kiss had gotten to her, no matter how she'd like to pretend it didn't. And really, did she think she could get to him with a few playful barbs to his male ego? If so, she had another thing coming. There may be a few things he was unsure about—his writing, his ability to continue to be relevant in the music industry, his music—but his manhood? Never in question.

"What's so funny?"

He looked up to see Derrek walking in from the front of the house. Brent shook his head, glad his friend had such impeccable timing. He hitched his thumb toward DJ's retreat. "Who got up and pissed in her Wheaties? Is she always like that?"

Derrek laughed. "Nah, not usually, but her truck broke down again this morning, and even though she knows she needs a new one, she's being stubborn about it."

Brent nodded. "Oh, must be a Diaz trait."

Derrek's lips quivered.

It was nice to see a smile this early in the day instead of a frown, even if Derrek's entrance didn't cause Brent's heart to race.

Derrek had the look of a man who'd been up for a while. His hair was sticking straight up, his clothes rumpled, and dark whiskers shadowed his cheeks. Seriously, the man looked like hell. "How about you and I go riding for old time's sake? I can't tell you how long it's been since I've been on a horse. We could go out this weekend, ride to Broken Creek, and pack a few beers and some sandwiches. What do you say?"

Derrek sighed and rubbed the back of his neck with his

hand. "God, those were good days. We'd pack our fishing poles and a six pack of beer and be gone all day."

Brent smiled at the memories. That was when life had been simpler. Even though he loved what he did now, he missed those days. Too bad there was no way he could have a little of both. "Some of my fondest memories took place down at the creek."

"Some of your fondest memories were with Shelly what's-her-face down at the creek," Derrek countered.

Brent didn't even bother to look ashamed. "Well, that's true. So, what do you say? You game?"

Derrek looked around as if seeing the mile long to-do list in his head and sighed. "I really wish I could. It's just..."

Brent was having none of it. His friend looked to be in dire need of some downtime, and that's what Brent did best —make people have a good time.

"It's just what? You have work to do? People are expecting an email, a phone call, a horse? Come on, what's the point of being the boss if you can't set your own schedule? Or, wait, do you have to ask DJ first before you can go?"

Brent knew the last comment was a low blow, but he was trying to get a reaction.

Derrek didn't take the bait. "Whatever, dude. Have you ever had to goad me into playing hooky?"

Brent gave his first full smile of the day. "Come to think of it, you never had to be pushed too hard. So is that a yes? This Friday night?"

Derrek got his traveler's mug out and went over to the coffee pot. Finding it empty, he groaned out loud. Man, Brent had never seen anyone go through the caffeine like the Diazes. What Derrek and DJ needed was a decent nap.

Brent responded, "Fine, this Friday. I'll meet you in front of the barn at three o'clock and don't be late because even though I don't need my sister's permission, I'd rather avoid the lecture."

Brent did a mock salute, secretly happy that his best friend blowing off Friday afternoon's work would royally piss off DJ. He almost couldn't wait to see the look on her face. Of course, he'd watch that said look from a distance, preferably from behind the window of the bunkhouse, but still.

FIVE

*T*he harsh rap on the door penetrated the deep fog of sleep that had claimed him like a loyal dog would his master. He fought his way awake, but even when he opened his eyes, clarity didn't descend. With the door opened and sunlight bursting in like a gunshot, he still had a hard time putting together that he was sleeping on a small double bed, rough cotton sheets, cold concrete floors, and depressingly beige walls.

Had he died and hell was a perpetual stay at Motel 6?

Then his eyes focused on the woman standing at the foot of his bed, and he realized he'd gotten it all wrong. He wasn't in hell after all.

The halo of sun that shown out from around her was just like the glow that would illuminate Wonder Woman between the pages of a graphic novel. Though, this super hero didn't wear a leotard and gold bracelets, but she did have a rope and a wicked looking Stetson in place of a gold head band.

"Rise and shine, Rock Star."

He squinted his eyes against the brightness, already

recognizing the voice. The all too mocking quality could belong to none other than DJ Diaz. "Couldn't keep away, huh? All the ladies eventually succumb," he mumbled in her general direction.

He'd only been here three days and already his plan of not obsessing over her was failing as quickly as his latest album. His priority needed to be writing his next single, not deigning to the wishes of a diehard kill-joy.

"My truck broke down again, and Derrek had to tow it to the shop, so I'm down a man. And since this here's a working ranch and everyone pulls his or her own weight, I need the manpower. Time to rise and shine." She tapped the rope against the side of her leg, and he wouldn't put it past her to use it on him if she didn't think he was moving fast enough. The thought was strangely appealing.

Brent ran his hand over his face and glanced toward the window. "It's barely light out," he whined. It'd been a long time since he'd gotten up before noon, and he was still on his L.A. schedule—up all night and sleep all day. Apparently, Miss Stick-up-her-rear-end wasn't down with that. He was a grown man, and no one-hundred-twenty-pound woman would be bossing him around. "Either take off your clothes and get into bed with me, or go away altogether. I had a late night. Besides, Derrek told you to back off. I'm here to work on my album—not on your ranch."

"A little advice, Rock Star, you *so* have to work on your pick up lines, but right now, I don't have time for your games. Derrek told me you haven't written crap since you came here. So, if you're not writing, you're working, I don't give a damn about what time you went to bed last night; I just want you out there helping me out. If any more horses of mine come down with hoof disease, there's not going to be a roof for you to quote-unquote work under." She reached over, grabbed his blanket, and pulled it off of with a snap.

There was a loud gasp that had him smiling.

Yeah, babe, I sleep naked.

He did the only thing a man who was completely confident in his manliness would do in a situation like this—he put his hands behind his head and nodded.

Her cheeks flamed red, and she quickly turned around. "Oh my God, I didn't know... I mean... I didn't mean... But... but... who the hell sleeps naked in a bunkhouse on a ranch full of people?"

"Rock stars, baby." Okay, he really wasn't that much of a prima donna, but there was no way he'd give up this opportunity to throw her nickname of him back in her face. Of course, he'd pay for that little comment later, but he knew it would be totally worth it.

She lowered her head and put her hands on her hips as if controlling her temper, and for one blessed moment he thought that kissing her wasn't the only way to render her speechless.

"If you don't stop reminding me that you front a boy band..." her pitch was as grating to the ear as a beginner strumming on a poorly tuned guitar. "...then I'll take the branding iron to you myself. Now get up. You've missed breakfast, so I'll meet you outside."

DJ walked out, letting the door slam loudly behind her. She kept her eyes straight ahead and didn't deviate from her path until she'd gotten to the back side of the stables where she'd be assured a degree of privacy. Only then did she turn toward the wall and lower her burning face in her hands.

Oh. My. God. Had she really just walked into Brent's room and stripped the sheets off a naked man? What the hell was wrong with her? How stupid. *How embarrassing.* And yet, even as her face burned and she doubted she'd ever be able to look him in the eye again, her mind replayed the vision of him in bed like a full-screen movie.

So he must do a little bit more than just prance around onstage and pick at his guitar. He was fit. She swallowed, surprisingly so. His chest was wide, shoulders broad, and even without touching him, she was sure she could add "hard" to the description. His stomach was flat, with a shadow of corded muscles underneath the skin that she knew, if flexed, would define a six pack. But what had been interesting were the intricate tattoos that curled around his biceps and over one broad shoulder, and the scripted stanza on the inside of his right forearm that had her dying of curiosity. What would an egotistical playboy have to say that was important enough to be permanently inked on his body?

And then... and then there was the other... the *lower*. DJ plucked at her shirt and blew down her chest to cool her skin that had nothing to do with the heat of the day. Okay, so he just might have a reason to brag. Maybe all those rumors hadn't been an exaggeration. He'd been, um... impressive, and this coming from a woman who worked with horses all her life.

Ugh. She picked her head up. No, she couldn't go there. There was only one thing she hated more than a lazy man, and that was a womanizing, lazy man. So yeah, while fantasizing about a handsome singer with rock hard abs and a dangerous smile was a fun way to waste a morning, it wasn't how she wanted to waste her day. She'd gotten used to being alone years ago, and a lonely heart was much better than a broken one. The sooner Brent left, the better, and there was no way to make a lazy man leave faster than request an honest day's work out of him.

DJ let her gaze wander over the fenced off pasture, where two of her horses grazed side by side, and the small dirt road that cut its way through the grass and disappeared over a sloping hill. She shook her head. She'd always prided herself on being honest, and her assessment of him wasn't totally fair. He hadn't become a country rock legend by luck alone. He'd always taken his music seriously. When they'd all been younger, he'd pretty much had that damn guitar strapped to his chest at all times. He'd written out lyrics on paper napkins, and made her and Derrek listen to the same song over and over again just so he could hear the change up or a particular guitar riff.

But that was Brent, all or nothing. The only thing that ever had mattered to him was his music. That was what he lived and breathed, and no one—and she meant no one— came a close second. Especially her.

The memory still hurt, even after all these years. Stupid. She should've been over his rejection, but that summer had been the worst time in her life.

She'd been young and impressionable. At fifteen, she'd been too young not to fall in love, and Brent at eighteen should've known better than to mess with his best friend's little sister. Brent was her first kiss. She couldn't say the same thing for him. It happened out of the blue. Even in her wildest dreams, she would've never believed he had thought of her like that. It was a week before Brent and Derrek graduated, and Brent already had plans to leave for Nashville after the ceremony, so her family threw them an early graduation party.

The mood might have been from the sentimental undercurrents of that night, or the beer her parents had allowed the boys to drink after the majority of the guests had gone home. Either way, it was a prime setting for a heartbreaker.

Brent had found her sitting on the stairs in her house. The downstairs was dark, and her parents had already turned in. They saw no need to chaperone, since she was the only girl left, and Derrek would be sure to look after her. The rest of the soon-to-be graduates were outside around the fire, laughing and telling crude jokes—no place for a fifteen year old girl. Danielle should've turned in, but she was too wired to sleep. Her whole world teetered on the cusp of change, excitement was in the air, and she was afraid to sleep in case she missed something. Brent was leaving for Nashville, and Derrek had a full ride scholarship to Texas State. Her cousin Emilio, who had been living with them for the last few years, had already signed up for the military and was preparing to ship out later this month. All the men in her life were leaving, and she couldn't help feeling left out.

"Hey, what's with the sad face?"

She'd looked up. Brent had one booted foot on the bottom step and a bottle of beer dangling in his left hand. He'd always been a good looking guy: blond hair, blue eyes, tall, athletic build; but tonight his eyes held a wild look he normally reserved for other girls.

She looked away. Her face showed everything she was feeling, and she didn't want him to see how thrilled she was for him to be talking to her. He sat down next to her, not a step away, not up against the wall, but right next to her, hip to hip, arm to arm. His jean-clad leg brushed up against her bare one. His plaid shirt still held the scent of the fire.

"You're pretty, you know that?"

She knew it was a tired, over-used line, he knew it was a

tired and over-used line, but it didn't matter. The way his voice caressed the words and his gaze heated her body made the words work. She wanted to believe him, so she did. From one heartbeat to the next, her body responded, and her breath grew shallow.

His languishing gaze traveled over her like a man with all the time in the world, while she couldn't wait until his mouth came down and touched hers. She was ready to rocket head long into the stars, his kiss the only thing keeping her firmly rooted to the earth.

She'd never been kissed before, but he was slow and a good teacher. He took his time coaxing her mouth open, nibbling at her lips. She remembered the taste of beer and the sweetness of the BBQ, the thick fullness of his hair when she grew bold enough to touch him, and the woodsy, smoky smell with the bite of aftershave underneath. She remembered how he pulled her into his lap, and how he'd chuckled when he tried to end the kiss, only for her to pull him back down and not let him go.

His mouth hovered right above the top button of her shirt. Her skin heated from his breath alone. When his hand rubbed her back through the thin layer of her cotton shirt, shocks of current ran through her body. Her heartbeat skipped, her legs tightened around his waist as small moans escaped from the back of her throat.

They stayed like that—her legs straddling his waist, his hands grabbing her behind—for what felt like days, but could've only been moments. He was the one to break it off.

"Danielle, Danielle honey, we've got to stop." His voice strained, his breath was fast and heated against her flushed skin.

Stop? Why stop? She'd never felt like this before, never

dreamed that she could float amongst the stars with just the touch of his lips against hers.

He rested his forehead against hers, his thumbs bracketing her mouth. "Don't give me a look like that. You should never give a guy like me a look like that." He blew out a sigh and rubbed his thumb over her lip. "Damn, Danielle, I had no idea...I..." he cleared his throat. "You know that I'm leaving in the morning?"

She nodded. He'd have to pry her arms from around his body before she'd let him go.

He took a strand of hair and brushed it across his lips. "So what I'm trying to say is, save that look, you know, save... this, for a guy who's going to be around. For a guy who's better than me. Do you understand what I'm saying?"

She nodded that she did, but it was already too late. He was the guy that she wanted to save her look for. He was the guy that was worth the wait. But then, she hadn't been old enough to know that this kiss was just a game, and that love and lust were not the same. A day later he was gone, and two weeks later her parents were dead.

And he never even came back for her parents' funeral.

DJ shook her head to bring her back to the present and wiped at the dampness in her eyes. It was silly to cry over something that had happened so long ago, but the memories of Brent and her parents' death were so intertwined that it was hard not to think of one without the other. That summer marked the hardest period in her life, and even after all these years, she missed her parents desperately. The one thing that had saved her was the ranch. It was hard to cry yourself to sleep after working fourteen hour days with no end in sight.

For ten years, she'd kept her head down and buried herself in her work. Those first few years had been the loneliest of her life, but bemoaning the past was worthless. She had a ranch to keep from going under, and she sure didn't need some gorgeous, full-of-himself guy stirring up desires for things she'd long since given up on. That was why she couldn't get drawn in with his mind-blowing kisses and overt come-ons. Her heart had shattered that summer, and she didn't need to repeat the process to realize that she had no desire to go through that again.

Because he would. Brent would love her and leave her, and she just couldn't be left behind again.

SIX

*B*rent was still rolling up his sleeves as he walked out of the bunkhouse. The morning air didn't quite have the bite of heat to it, but the clear, cloudless blue sky promised another hot one. He saw DJ standing in the front entrance of the stables, a cowboy hat on her head and a shovel in her hand. Arms darkened from years in the sun, ponytail in a thick, long, tangled mess down her back. If she was embarrassed about what had happened in his bedroom, she sure didn't look like it. Instead, she had a determined tilt to her head, her stance screaming *all business*.

Too bad; there'd been a moment in the bunkhouse when he thought he'd glimpsed desire in her eyes. They could've had some fun, but she wouldn't know what a good time was, even if it walked over and hit her upside the head. He came up from behind her. "Your servant, here at your command."

At the sound of his voice, she startled and turned around.

He didn't like alarming her. He touched her arm to settle her. "Sorry, I didn't mean to scare you."

"You didn't; I was just lost in thought." She looked him up and down, but didn't pull her arm away. "It's going to be hot out today. You sure that you want to wear a long sleeve shirt?"

No, he wasn't sure, but he hadn't really packed clothes suitable for a ranch hand, and he didn't want to see that condescending smile on her face when he asked to borrow one of Derrek's. He'd do that later, when DJ wasn't around to arch that judgmental brow at him. He knew she would never let him live it down if he wore the only other thing he packed—a silk button down—to muck out stalls. He shrugged. "I'll be fine."

She shrugged back. "Your heat stroke." Then started down the wide aisle between the stables. He followed her, noticing some water damage from the leaky roof and some stall walls propped up with some shoddy workmanship. Things were slipping, and even though the horses looked well taken care of, he could tell the ranch was barely holding its own.

"I need you to muck out the stalls," she continued. "Sweep them clean, and then put fresh hay down that's been specially treated with an antibiotic."

He nodded. "Which ones?"

She gave him a queer look. "All of them."

Brent looked around and took in the concrete floor littered with random bits of hay, and the white-painted wood doors that marked each stall. He did a mental count. "That's twelve stalls!"

He couldn't see her eyebrows, but he was pretty sure they were high up under her hat in a "you're an idiot" expression she wore so well. "I'm well aware of how many stalls I have."

"Do I get any help?"

"Hmmm..." She glanced around as if looking for another ranch hand, than pinned him with that no nonsense black stare of hers. "Maybe I'm not explaining myself well enough. You," she said, a pointy finger stabbing his chest, "are the help."

She handed him the shovel and pointed toward the wheelbarrow. Then she patted him on the cheek in a condescending gesture. "Oh, and Brent, make sure to drink plenty of water, I know you're not used to working in the sun, and I wasn't kidding about the sun-stroke."

———

Holy freaking cow, his back was on fire, and his fingers were throbbing with blisters. He closed the last stall door and leaned against it to catch his breath. He'd just finished up his last stall, which was good, since he could no longer feel his arms. Sure, he worked out; a guy couldn't be a country crossover heart-throb with a beer belly and man boobs. But doing this type of work made him aware of muscles he hadn't known existed.

And not to mention the heat. When did Texas get so bloody hot? Or had he just come to visit the Double D ranch in the middle of a heat wave? He'd lost his long-sleeved shirt around stall number five, and he was pretty sure at stall ten his underwear had gotten soaked through. But the important thing was that he'd done it. He couldn't wait to see DJ's face when he told her. She of little faith probably thought he wouldn't make it through half the stalls.

Just then he saw her walking past, her hat low down to shade her eyes while she was busy talking on the phone. "Yes, yes, Gus. I got it, the truck is shot. I know it's the same thing you always say and I'm telling you just get her up and running. I have horses to deliver, and I need my truck."

There was a pause in the conversation as she stopped walking and used her boot to kick a rock in the dirt. Brent had no idea what was happening at the other end, but by the look on her face, she didn't like what she was hearing.

"Well, you'd better not have told Derrek that the brakes need replacing. I'd never hear the end of it. I promise the next payment I get will go toward new brakes, but I need my truck to make the money, so get it done."

She ended the conversation and shoved her phone into her back pocket. From his vantage point, Brent could see the lines of fatigue that creased her brow and the heavy slump of her shoulders. Something unfamiliar tugged at his heart. He didn't like the sound of this conversation. For siblings who were as close as these two, it was odd how much they kept from each other. It was like each was so afraid of worrying the other. What had been Derrek's concern about his little sister? He didn't want her to grow old on this ranch before her time. What were Derrek's exact words? Get her to work less and play more. Problem was, with that pursed, uptight expression on her face, she didn't look like she wanted to play. Good thing Brent loved a challenge. He'd never come across a woman he couldn't bend just a little.

DJ started to walk again, head down, fingers massaging the crease between her two brows. He must've made some noise as he started towards her, because DJ looked up just in time to avoid running into him. She jumped back, and he caught her elbow to steady her.

"I seem to be catching you off guard a lot today. Must mean my presence is putting you on edge." He did his full smile, liking the way her gaze kinda stuck on his bare chest.

Oh, had he forgotten to put his shirt back on? Stupid him. "I finished all the stalls."

"Wow." Her gaze finally found his face. "And it only took you all day to finish a half-day's worth of work. Lucky you."

Why was it that when she narrowed her gaze and shot him a look that said he wasn't worth her time of day his blood started pumping? Maybe because he could see right through her BS. And the fact her gaze had fallen to his chest again. He tightened his gut for good measure. "So, I was thinking you and I should go down to the creek and take a quick swim before dinner."

That took her off guard. Her eyes widened, and her mouth dropped. Well... better than contempt. "Why would I ever do that?"

He was still touching her, so he let his hand move up to caress her arm. He liked the feel of muscle underneath her soft skin and how she looked down at his hand and then back up as if questioning his nerve. He smirked. Almost worth killing himself on her damn ranch. "Because it's hot outside, because it's fun, because you could spend time with me."

Modesty had never been his strong suit.

She shook her head, her face angling up toward his. Her eyes narrowed and that famous black-eyed gaze got his breath quickening better than any physical labor could. "Again, why would I ever do that?"

He removed his hat and pushed his sweat-drenched hair off his face, then placed his Stetson back at just the right angle.

"Really? After laboring in the hot sun you're still going to cut me off at the knees?" His voice was the perfect blend of sweet and spicy, tangy and tart that rolled off his tongue like five-star cuisine. "Don't I deserve a little incentive for doing all that work?"

"Oh, yes, absolutely." She nodded as if in total agreement. He didn't buy that for one nanosecond. "I appreciate all your hard work. So, in return, I'll give you a roof over your head and some food in your belly."

She let her head tilt to the side and rested one hand on her hip. Her cockiness didn't scare him at all.

He took a step closer. They were almost touching. Could she feel the energy crackling between them? He knew he couldn't take her by surprise like he had before. This time he'd have to woo her. "So what? No swim? We could skinny dip."

She smiled. More at his audacity than at him, but he'd take it. "No swim."

He wasn't about to stop there. "How about a kiss, then?"

She shook her head, gaze heavenward as if asking for strength. "I'm speechless."

He raised one eyebrow and smiled his half grin. "I have that effect on women."

She laughed, but she didn't say no. That was always a good sign. He tipped his head down and let the brim of their two hats meet. He wanted other parts of them to meet also.

"Come on." He leaned in closer, loving how much taller he was. Loving how she seemed small and delicate in his presence. Her scent of hard work, sunshine, and fresh hay floated up around him. "When do you ever get the chance to kiss a country legend? Isn't it every girl's fantasy to kiss a rock star? I'm just helping you knock something off your bucket list."

Her lips continued their upward slant. She might just be enjoying this as much as he was. "I thought I already did that. But I'm not like other girls. I don't like rock stars, and I don't like cocky, full-of-themselves men."

"But you like kisses," he countered.

She eyed him warily, but he took great pains in noticing that she hadn't backed up or slapped him yet. Good signs, good signs. "Yes," she said. Was it just him, or was her voice a bit on the husky side?

"Great, I can work with that. One out of three isn't bad."

"Really?" She tipped her head back to look him in the eye. Her smile was wide and full now. "Wow. By my calculations, that's thirty-three percent, which is basically failing."

He groaned and threw his hands up. "Did you just throw a math problem into a conversation about kissing? You really do have a problem. Okay, I'll tell you what, give me five minutes of kissing, and see if I don't change your mind."

"Five minutes?" Her eyebrows shot skyward and jaw dropped as if he'd asked for five days instead. "Five minutes is a looooong time."

He shook his head. His turn to be surprised. "Five minutes is a drop in the bucket. You've already spent ten here debating the issue."

"And that's why I don't have five more." She started to turn to go, but he caught her arm to make her stay.

Time to pull out all the stops. "Because I'm that good, I'll kiss you for three. I'm pretty sure I can rock your world in three." *Pretty sure?* What the hell was he saying? He was slipping. Must be the heat. "No, I'm sure. Three is all I need."

She hesitated as if thinking it over, then she licked her lips and held up two fingers. "Two, and my world stays solidly on its axis."

"Done." He wasted no time. His hands reached up and encircled her neck, his thumbs stroking the underside of her jaw. He bent his head and found those juicy full lips he'd been staring at the whole time. He made himself go slow. He was good at what he did and kissing was something that shouldn't be rushed.

He nipped at the corners of her mouth, drew a line with his tongue across her bottom lip. Her lips were soft and plump, her mouth wide and sexy as hell. He'd known all this from before, but what he hadn't expected was that kissing her was the same feeling he got when he wrote a great lyric or perfected the best chorus. Kissing her, her taste riding his tongue, was like experiencing the only passion he'd ever known—pouring out his music in front of hundreds of fans.

He wasn't sure who pulled away first, but they both were breathless, and she was clinging to him like the earth had just shook.

He recovered first. "A little off-balance?" He couldn't help but grin.

"Oh, I thought I was holding you up." She disentangled herself from his arms, readjusted her hat, and began to swagger away.

"You know, DJ, I would've been able to do that in one. " He called after her, loving the new bounce in her step.

"And you know what, Brent," she said, with no backward glance, but just a tell-off wave of her fingers instead. "I would've let you go for five."

He groaned in a dramatic fashion and clutched at his heart. Eat your heart out ladies, he'd just fallen in love—all over again.

SEVEN

*D*J's bare feet padded across the tiled floor as she headed to the kitchen. She'd just gotten out of the shower and had donned a pair of soft sweats and a sleeveless cami—basically her pj's. It was only seven o'clock, and she was pretty much ready for bed. She wondered what Brent would say about her turning in so early. She sure didn't keep rock star hours.

She passed the living room and noticed a pair of socked feet propped up on the arm of the couch and a long, lean body stretched out among the throw pillows and afghans tossed across the back. Her brother was out for the night, so that long, cool drink of water could only be Brent. What the hell?

She thought Derrek had restricted Brent to the bunkhouse. Didn't he have a couch and a TV to laze around in there? She turned heel and started back up the stairs, then stopped. This was ridiculous. This was her house, so why was she the one sneaking around? The truth was, after the, um... *incident* by the stables a day ago, she'd basically avoided him. That had been harder than she'd first thought.

He was supposed to stay at the bunkhouse, but what she hadn't expected was that he'd shown up every morning to help around the ranch. He'd volunteered for whatever needed to be done, no matter how menial. He worked until she sent the ranch hands home and then holed up in the bunkhouse. Sometimes, when she couldn't sleep—which was becoming more and more common—she'd go out to check on the horses, and she'd hear him strumming one chord or another, plugging away.

The fact that this was the first night that he wasn't in his bunkhouse on his guitar was a concern. She'd thought he'd gotten over his writer's block. As much as she had said to the contrary, she really did want him to succeed. She wanted him to be happy; she just wanted him to be happy away from here. Away from her.

His being under her roof, underfoot, was just too much. He was just too good looking, too damn charming, and made her laugh more than she had in years. The fact of the matter was it was harder and harder to pretend she didn't care. It was too easy to get used to his being here. Too easy to forget that he was going to leave, just like he did back then, like he would when his album was finished.

DJ sighed. This was ridiculous. *The best way to get over your fears is to confront them.* She headed back to the living room and plopped down on the overstuffed chair across from Brent. His worn guitar was propped up against the side table, a cold bottle of beer sweating without the benefit of a coaster. She resisted the urge to pick up the bottle and swipe at the condensation with her hand. Instead, she cut her gaze away and looked over at him. He'd glanced up at her entrance, his dreamy blue gaze peeking over the cover of a hard-backed book.

"You read?"

His brows shot up and hid behind the scruffiness of his sandy blonde hair.

Okay, that didn't come out right. She wasn't here to pick a fight. What she meant was, Oh...you read?—the tone emphasizing the positive not the negative. She was just surprised. He didn't seem to be the type to appreciate literature. Of course, there seemed to be a lot of assumptions about Brent that didn't quite fit anymore. Damn, she hated to be wrong.

"You just think I'm a dumb country singer? All good looks and no brains?" He smiled when he said it, as if goading her into acknowledging how good looking he was.

She didn't have to be goaded. He was hot—with his shaggy blond hair that brushed at his collar and fell across his forehead in that perfected wind-swept look. With those bedroom blue eyes that held the promise of sin and redemption all at the same time. With that tall, rock hard body that filled out a pair of jeans and a plaid button-down like nobody's business. Yeah, he was hot. Too bad he knew it.

She chose to ignore his comment and instead threw out a goad of her own. "Shouldn't you be writing some lyrics or something instead of reading..." she peered forward to read the title on the cover, "*Pride and Prejudice*? Really?"

His smile faded, and he let the book plop down on his chest. He scrubbed one hand over his beautiful face. From this angle she could see a light dusting of whiskers on his cheek. Funny, he could never grow a full-on beard, not with that blond hair. "I'm... I'm working on that. Just taking a little breather."

She nodded, not at all buying his line. She knew procrastination when she saw it. She swung her legs over the arm of the chair and started to bounce her foot in the air. Maybe she could use this to her advantage. "So... ah... what's the book about?"

He looked down at the book on his chest and then back at her. His expression a mixture of confusion and disbelief.

Her face heated, and she cleared her throat. "I mean... I was just wondering. I haven't had a chance to read it, is all, and I was hoping you could, you know, give me the cliff note version."

"Of *Pride and Prejudice*? Of this book?" He pointed a finger to the cover, the sensual grin perpetually on his face slipping into an opened-mouth gaping.

"Yes," she snapped. Okay, she might be getting a little defensive. What was the big deal? No one's read every book out there. "Do you see another book lying around?"

His hand came up to cover his mouth as if to keep myriads of words behind his closed lips. Why bother now? It wasn't like he'd ever kept his opinion to himself before. "It's just that this is a classic, and I don't think I've met a woman who hasn't read *Pride and Prejudice* before."

Reading wasn't really her thing. She'd always been too wired to sit still for long. Reading took patience, and that, according to her brother, was something she was severely lacking. "Listen," she said, feeling the need to defend herself, which was ridiculous considering who she was defending herself to, "it wasn't required reading in school, and I've been busy."

He shook his head. "Not even the movie?"

Why had she come in here? She should've just gone to bed. She shrugged. "I must've missed it in the theaters."

"All six times? Not even the BBC mini-series?"

She threw her hands up in defeat, totally irritated now. "Okay, can we establish that yes, I don't know what *Pride and Prejudice* is about? Listen, Derrek is always on me about working too much. He said I didn't have much of a social life—"

Brent snorted.

She glared at him. "Listen, I don't need another man throwing his opinion about my life into the mix. One's enough, thank you very much."

Brent just arched a brow and waited. How could he look so good in nothing but one of Derrek's old shirts and a pair of ratty jeans? She sighed, suddenly feeling self-conscious about how her wet hair looked and wondering if she should've taken more time to comb through it or not.

"Anyway, he signed me up for this book club with a bunch of women." She fingered her hair. Why did she suddenly care if she looked a mess or not? "Can you just cut me some slack? Book club meets next week, and I haven't even started the damn thing. I just need a general outline."

He smirked, his face so genuine-fake that it was humorous. "You know I'm always at your assistance. All you need to do is ask."

"Right," she smirked back. "Because that's the first thing that comes to mind when I think of you—helpful."

He swung his legs around and sat, leaning forward on the edge of the couch. "So you think of me? How often?"

She would not reward him with a laugh. She wouldn't. "The book, Rock Star. Focus."

He slumped back into that casual, relaxed style of his with that damn self-satisfied smile riding his lips again. "Okay, a general outline. It's basically about a man who has a lot of prestige. He's well off, from the upper crust of society. Some think he is a bit full of himself, you know, prideful, maybe borderline arrogant."

"Oh," she gestured with her hand. "So he's like... like a rock star."

He smirked. "Yes, but a good-looking rock star."

"Of course. Is there any other kind?" Only under threat of torture would she admit that his self-confidence was a total turn-on. How could anyone be so sure of themselves? So at ease in their own skin?

"Glad we agree." He threw his arms along the back of the couch and let his head rest back. "So, the heroine, her family isn't as well off, but she's from a genteel family. Money's an issue."

"I like her already. We have so much in common." She crossed her arms over her chest when she felt her nipples tighten. Must be from the AC after a hot shower, nothing whatsoever to do with him.

"Sure. She's exactly like you—without the temper, the mouth, or the attitude, but yeah, very similar." He nodded his head, seemingly getting into the conversation.

She blew off his character assessment with a roll of her eyes. "Say no more, I already know what happens, they fall madly in love and live happily ever after."

He sighed and did an eye roll of his own. "Leave it to you to skip all the best parts. If you go right to the end you miss all the fun, but that's your M.O., right?"

"That's what I've been trying to get you to do—tell me all the best parts," she said, completely ignoring his ongoing complaint about her.

His eyes twinkled and that in no way meant anything good for her. "The part where the heroine realizes that she's lost without the hero and falls to her knees and asks if she can do the hero a favor by performing wild and earth shattering maneuvers in bed."

Her eyes widened, and she repeated her promise not to encourage his bad behavior. "Really? And then what does the hero do?"

He grabbed his beer off the end table and took a sip, she guessed to help keep a straight face. "Well, then he complies. He had to. He's the hero, after all."

"Hmmm, wasn't this book set in the eighteen-hundreds? Not so sure that was the norm."

An eyebrow cocked in disbelief. "So you don't know what the book is about, but you know when it was written?"

She shrugged. "I got to the first page."

"Well, for your information, they had sex in the eighteen-hundreds."

"True, but they didn't write about it."

He shrugged his shoulder. "Sounds like you don't believe me. You could always read the book for yourself. Then we could compare notes. Or..." He leaned forward, elbows on knees, voice lowering into sexy-hush, as if to lure her in with a secret. She wouldn't tell him his ploy was working. "I could just tell you in explicit detail about how the heroine took off her clothes, knelt before the hero, and begged him to let her—."

She swung her legs around and mirrored his position, cutting him off. Two could play at this game. "Wow, *begged*. Very self-sacrificing of the heroine."

He shifted so that her legs were captured between his. A forward move, maybe even a tad aggressive, but it was a dangerous game they were playing, and she had no desire to call a retreat. "Oh yes," his voice the same sexy rich tone he used when he sang love songs. "It was a *very* heroine thing to do."

She rested her chin on her palm and looked up at him from under her lashes. She wasn't completely socially challenged; she did know how to flirt. "I think you and I have differing ideas about what is a *very* heroine thing to do."

He grabbed her fingers with his free hand and brought

them to a quick brush against his lips. "Or we could just skip all the fiction parts and go straight on through to the real thing."

That got her; she laughed. She had to in order to cover up the jolt of excitement that rushed through her at his gesture. "So let me get this straight, you're asking me to get naked and play a casual game of 'hide the salami' with you?"

"Ouch. You make it sound so crass." He leaned back as if wounded. "If you just add a few flowery words, we could call this whole thing a romance. I, of course," he nodded to show his complete agreement, "wouldn't decline the offer either way."

There was a moment, a fraction of a second, when Brent thought she was going to take him up on his offer. Okay, not really, but his body responded as if there was a definite hope.

Her lush mouth tilted up in a come-hither smile, while her eyes shot him lasers of disdain. That's what drove him nuts about her, and consequently made her irresistible to him—the mixed signals she threw him. Did she like him? Was he making any progress? He'd rather she kiss him or slap him, but either way he'd know where he stood with her.

She reached over and plucked his beer from his grasp— wisps of hair drying about her face, scents of vanilla and lilacs tantalized him. There was a slight sheen on her lips left over from when she licked them, cheeks still flushed from her recent shower.

He swallowed. She was so close. *Please please please*. Just lean over and he'd take care of the rest.

She took a sip of beer and then let her arms cross over her captured legs. Her shirt gapped, and he could tell she wasn't wearing a bra. "So why are you here?" she asked.

What? Hadn't they just been talking about whether she was going to go to bed with him or not? "What do you mean?"

"I mean, why are you here? What are you doing hiding out at my ranch? You could be at some resort surrounded by all your peeps and adoring fans. So why here, where you're getting up before dawn and I'm making you earn your keep?"

No, no, let's go back to the previous conversation. "Right." He tried his best to squelch his disappointment. "No one's lazy around here."

She smiled, and he studied her face to see if it reached her eyes. "That's right. This isn't Fort-Worth. We actually work our ranch."

He inhaled slowly in an attempt to control his breathing. He wondered what she'd do if he flung her down on the couch and kissed her silly. They were finally in a place that he could do more than just kiss. Getting her shirt off would be great, for starters. "So you don't know anything about *Pride and Prejudice*, but you're up on eighties soap operas?"

She threw her head back and took a long pull from the bottle. He was so proud that he didn't groan out loud. He had it bad. "When the soap opera is based in Dallas, you betcha. You still haven't answered my question. What's your agenda here?"

"I'm writing."

"You could write anywhere," she countered.

But you're here.

Where the hell had that thought come from? Yes, he could write anywhere, but the truth was he hadn't. Not for a long time. His manager had called him last night. Different night, same conversation. Sure, Brent said all the right things. It's coming, it's on the way, almost done, just a few more tweaks. But the truth was, he hadn't gotten close to writing a song. He tried, but nothing came... His muse had up and left him, like he'd been a cheating boyfriend.

The truth, he was scared. Scared that he'd lost his way. Scared that at twenty-seven his career was already over, that he was already just some washed up country singer, and a freaking joke in the industry. That's why he'd come back. This was his last-ditch effort to find his passion again and write his album. And if that didn't work, at least he'd fail with people around him who'd known him before he was a star—when he'd just been some loser with a guitar.

But he couldn't say any of this to DJ. Instead, he let her hand drop.

She shot him a searching gaze. "The questions only get more difficult from here on out, so..."

"I'm here to write. I need to finish up my album, that's all." He sat back and picked up his guitar.

"I don't understand you, Brent." She shook her head. "You always had that damn guitar in your hand when we were growing up. What's the problem now?"

The problem? The problem was that it was hard to write love songs when he was sexually frustrated, but he wisely kept that thought to himself. "Most days I wake up and the last thing I want to do is pick up this damn guitar. I'd rather watch TV, do the dishes, or work on your ranch. I'm just not in the mood to write. The pressure can be immense. It's hard."

She leaned back and again swung one leg over the arm

of the chair as if they were just two old friends catching up. "I hear you. I feel like that all the time."

"You do?" He couldn't believe it. She was one of the hardest workers he'd ever known. One of the most driven. "I'd never thought I'd hear that from you."

"Sure," she said, and then leaned back in the overstuffed chair and gazed at the ceiling. "I think about how I'm sick of running this ranch, sick of catering to these horses that seem to be costing me more and more, while people expect bargain-basement deals. How this economy is making it almost impossible for me to break even, much less make a living. Every day I think it's too hard. Some days I don't want to get up in the morning. And most days, I think I'd be happy doing just about anything else."

He sat up. She understood. Finally, someone was speaking his language. "Exactly! Yes. So when you feel like that, what do you do?"

She flipped her legs back around and leaned in real close. He supposed she didn't want him to miss her words, her expression, her meaning. She didn't have to worry. His entire attention was focused on what she was going to say next.

"I get up and do it anyways." She got up and ruffled his hair like she would a dog's, and then stopped and did something he would've never expected. She bent down and softly placed a kiss on top of his head. "That's why it's called work, Rock Star. Thanks for the beer."

EIGHT

*B*rent's cell phone buzzed an annoying jingle bells rhythm that had him barely cracking an eyelid. He threw the dinky pillow over his head, which did nothing to muffle the sound. If he ignored the phone, the person on the other end would surely get a clue and leave him alone.

Sand paper scratched behind his closed eyelids. His head hurt, back ached, and he didn't even know what time he'd finally gotten to bed last night. After DJ left him sexually frustrated and annoyed as hell at her parting... gesture, he'd gotten pissed. Who the hell did she think she was, telling him to get to work? He was the one who'd worked his butt off making a career out of something so many people had failed at. He'd played at all the skanky bars, all the local dives. Had even been homeless for a time, sleeping on people's couches just to get from one gig to another.

He sighed. No, it was time to get honest with himself. What had he been doing since his first single finally made it big? He'd been living off all those songs he'd written when he was younger. Sure, he'd been touring and signing autographs, but as for actually working, writing new material?

He'd stopped taking time to write, and instead went to parties and lived the high life.

When was the last time he'd put in a full night's work of writing? Well, he did last night. He'd wanted to show DJ that he wasn't just a pretty face with a guitar, and that he actually had some talent to back up his success. Finally, the muse had hit, and he'd found his chorus.

So you think that you know me?

Well, I'm here to tell you I'm more than just a pretty face and, this here, guitar.

I've got a whole lotta lovin' if you'd see your way past my lonely facade.

There were a few more verses that needed to be polished, but he'd gotten the chorus down and the beat was catchy. The sun had reached high noon by the time he'd finally sent the rough demo he recorded on his phone to his manager.

He'd fallen face first into bed with a raging headache and cramped fingers, but there'd been a self-satisfied smile on his face. He'd written a solid song for the first time in years, and damn, it felt good.

His phone buzzed again. He rolled back over and threw his arm over his ear, but it didn't help. The phone just started again as soon as the voice messaging picked up.

He groaned. No rest for the weary. He flipped over and grunted into the speaker, barely taking the time to swipe at the screen.

"Brent? Brent, is that you?"

He knew he should recognize the voice, but his brain just wasn't making the connection. "Who's this?"

"It's Sally. Wake the hell up!"

"Sally?" he yawned.

"Sally, your manager, who just listened to your next

number one song. How can you even be sleeping at a time like this?"

"What are you talking about?" He pushed himself up and began working on getting his eyes open. He really needed to get a coffee maker for the bunkhouse. One that had an automatic timer so he could wake up to the smell of liquid caffeine instead of the pile of dirty clothes in the corner and his work boots by the door.

"The sound bite you just sent me. Yeah, it's a little rough, but I love the chorus. This is something that we can totally work with. I'm so excited." Her voice sounded a little too chipper for this early in the morning.

"Good. Good." He scratched his leg, and covered the phone to mute a loud yawn. Damn sheets were as soft as goat's hair.

"I mean, this has heart," she said talking a mile a minute. She always talked fast, but it was even worse when she was excited. "This is something totally different from what you've done before. It's sharp, but soulful. Where did this come from?"

He couldn't tell her the source was the worse sexual frustration he'd had since adolescence. Or the desire to prove to a certain woman that he was worth more than she gave him credit for. "Umm, er... ahhh."

"You're at the ranch, right? With your friend in Texas?"

"Yes," he said, pinching himself to see if he was awake. Sally wasn't calling to yell at him? She was singing his praises instead? This must be a dream.

"Great. Well, whatever you're doing, it's working for you. You've got to take advantage of this roll."

What was Sally talking about? "What roll?"

"This writing roll you are on. You know as well as I do that your next album is long overdue. You've got to get some songs on the charts or your career will be part of the *has-beens*."

"Yeah, yeah, I know. I'm getting ready to go fishing with my buddy, but I should be on the flight out tomorrow morning. When I get home I'll buckle down and write after the promotion tour that's lined up next week. I promise. Oh, but then after that, I've got that overseas thing..."

Sally sighed. He could almost see her bright white hair spiked up in her usual sharp style. Her makeup would be minimal, but her skin was flawless, and even closing in on sixty she still was a beautiful woman. "You're not hearing what I'm saying." He pulled the phone away from his ear to tone down the shouting. Okay, here it was. Now he knew he wasn't dreaming.

"The most important thing for you to do is write your next album," she continued. "I've cancelled the promotion tour."

"What?" This got his full attention. "You can't do that. Those venues were booked for months."

"Those venues were small two-bit places that I didn't want you playing in the first place. I already talked to the Label and they agree. The most important thing is your next album."

Brent groaned. He knew everything she said was right. He needed to concentrate on writing his music. "Fine, but I can't stay here. I—"

She cut him off. "Of course you can. You need to get back to your roots. What's wrong?" Her voice was already pitched in concern. Sally always had an uncanny ability to know if one of her artists was having a problem. Annoying as hell, but very effective career wise. "Did you and your friend have a fight? Let me call and talk to him."

"What?" He was mortified at the thought. "No! I can

figure out this part of my life, thank you very much. I'm a grown man, Sally."

Sally was good, but once you let her manage one part of your life she tended to start taking over the other parts as well. Hence, the reason there was a personal trainer sent to his house on a daily basis. Damn sadist... the trainer, not Sally.

"Great, then it's settled. I'll expect six more songs like that one by when...?"

"I don't know. Give me like six months?"

"Great, you'll have it in my hands in four weeks. Keep sending me the sound bites. I want to hear you through the whole process." He could hear her tapping her long French manicured nails on the desk through the phone.

Brent groaned. "No, that's not going to work,"

"Why not?" she asked. "Are your parents giving you a hard time?"

Sally was somewhat familiar with the strained relationship with his parents. Even though he loved them very much and knew they only wanted the best for him, he'd never gotten over the fact that they didn't believe in him. Even now, they seemed to be worried that one day his career would blow up in his face, and he'd end up back home with them. He'd rather go homeless. Still, he made an effort to keep in touch and had called them the other day, and besides the awkwardness that had always been there, they were doing great. "It's not that."

"Then what is it?"

He sighed. "A certain person of the female variety."

"Do I need to get a restraining order? It's better to start the process now..." He could hear her typing in the background, already making notes to call the police station.

"What? No! If anything it's the other way around. She's

pretty much all I think about." He didn't want to tell Sally his erotic thoughts. There were some parts of his life he could manage by himself.

"Hmmm... well, that's interesting." There was a drawn out pause that signaled a quiet mind at work. "So it's her who's playing hard to get?"

He let his head fall into his hand and massaged the pain at his temples. "The problem is, I don't know if she's playing."

There was a loud *tsk* from the phone. "You're a country music star, for Pete's sake, of course she's playing."

"See," he slammed his palm on the bed. "That's what I keep saying, but she still turned me down flat."

"Then buy her something. I have the Lamar's jeweler on speed dial. Would you like me to order some pearls, or is this a diamond kinda thing?"

Brent closed his eyes and pictured DJ with a string of pearls around her neck, then a string of diamonds, and then nothing else except diamonds and pearls. He groaned. Really, if he hadn't coerced Derrek into going fishing this afternoon, he'd have booked a flight out today. This fantasizing thing was getting ridiculous. "That's not going to work."

What would DJ do with an expensive necklace? He could tell Sally was getting annoyed with his whining. She wasn't the only one. A thought came to him. "Do you know how much horsepower you would need to pull a trailer?"

It was her turn to be confused. "What?"

"Never mind. I'll figure it out. Thanks, Sally."

"New songs. Three weeks." There was no way she was getting off this phone without emphasizing her point.

"I thought you said four?"

"And I thought you said last year."

"Touché."

He hung up the phone and leaned back into bed. He didn't get why this was so hard. Women loved him. He loved women. He never had issues getting someone to hook up with him for a week or so. He treated his women well. Bought them stuff.

But DJ was different. She was so serious, and he was a charmer. And yet... the best thing for them both would be for him to keep his fishing plans with Derrek and then get on the first flight out of Texas. The thing DJ had done when she kissed him on the head like... like... He shook his head. The kiss more than scared him; it had rocked him to the core. Why? He groaned and pounded his fist into his pillow. Why? Because it felt real? Because it was the first thing that passed between them that wasn't about flirting and getting her into his bed? He liked to *fall* in love, but he didn't actually want to *be* in love. Those two things were totally different. One faded quickly, while the other. Well, the other had no place in his life.

And that kiss. That kiss felt more like the latter than the former. He had to remember that he already had a lover, and her name was music. And damn what a jealous witch she could be.

NINE

*T*he horse's lulling movements that encouraged Brent to pass out in the saddle finally stopped. The horse neighed softly and stomped his hoof, impatient to call it a night and head into the barn, making Brent decide it might be best to dismount.

Deciding to keep his eyes closed for the moment, he worked instead on unsticking his tongue from the roof of his mouth. When he could finally swallow, the taste of road-kill was almost enough to make him sick. He groaned and braved opening his eyes—this time to get an up close and personal sight of his horse's mane. He disengaged the death grip he had around the horse's neck and pushed himself upright in the saddle. He took a moment to look around. Where the hell was he? The motion-detector light from the back porch clicked on, allowing him to make out the bunk house, the barn doors, and the main house's back door. *What the....*

The memory of going out "fishing" with Derrek came back in a hazy wave. They might've drunk more than they fished, but that hadn't been his fault. If Derrek had just kept to the plan of a six pack and some sandwiches, they both would've been fine. *But noooo.* Derrek pulled out some fireball whiskey that tasted like candy and had gone down even smoother. The more they drank, the better Brent had felt, and before they knew it the whole bottle was gone.

An uneasy feeling nestled in his gut as he tried to piece the last few hours together. With the utmost care he turned around, hoping against all hope that Derrek would be sitting on his horse behind Brent.

Brent turned back around and stared straight ahead. He waited a moment, drew a deep breath to quell the dizziness, then took another look. Nope. Still the same. Derrek's horse was there, but no Derrek.

A string of choice words danced around in his head, but he was too drunk to utter them.

I'm soooo screwed.

The creek was about a mile and a half away in the middle of nowhere, and being this late, it was darker than midnight under a cast-iron skillet. He had no idea where Derrek had fallen off, and even worse, no real way to go after him. What he needed was to get Derrek's truck and slowly drive back the way they'd come to see if there was a passed out cowboy along the road.

Except he didn't know where Derrek's keys were, and even if he did, he didn't think he could even find the ignition in his condition.

Brent thought for a long hard moment. There had to be another option. There had to be another way. Except, for the life of him, he couldn't think of any way around going into the main house and asking DJ for help.

The thought jacked up the queasiness in his stomach. This was worse than getting booed off stage. This was worse than getting caught with his pants down around his ankles

by the paparazzi. For the record, that had only happened
once, and his agent was able to get the pictures down off the
Internet relatively quickly.

With little choice, Brent did his best to dismount. He
quickly found himself butt down in the dirt, foot still stuck
in the stirrup. Holy donkey balls, what was in that fireball
whiskey—morphine? He couldn't even feel his lips; how the
hell was he supposed to get his legs under him? He
unhooked his boot and crawled back to the horse to un-
cinch the saddle. This whole thing might take longer than
expected. At least one of them should be comfortable. With
Herculean effort, he pulled himself together and stumbled
toward the back door. Thank God it was unlocked. If the
door hadn't been, he didn't think he was up to figuring out a
plan B.

He stumbled through the dark house with relative ease.
It was basically a clear shot from the back door to the front
staircase. This wasn't the first night he'd stumbled around
the furniture a tad over-inebriated, and the decor hadn't
really changed much over the years. Something told him
that watching HDTV was not a pastime of DJ's. He paused
at the stairs and contemplated the challenge of the long,
steep staircase—what the hell, there was no one around to
see anyways—got down on his hands and knees and
crawled up. By some miracle he found himself on his feet
and in front of her bedroom door. He should've knocked.
There was something in the back of his brain that told him
to knock, but there was a louder voice that said he'd better
get this done quick before he found himself face down on
the carpet. He pushed the door open and waited for his eyes
to adjust.

They didn't. The room was freakishly dark and there
was a low whirling noise that sounded like a distant ocean,

but hell, it could very well be his own blood slogging slowly past his ears. His tongue felt alien, his lips twice the normal size. "DJ, wakth upf." He swallowed and tried again. "Dee Jaaayyy I've needs your helpth."

Nothing, just the soothing noise of a distant coast and a slight breeze of a ceiling fan. He stumbled to the side of the bed. Was that lump under the covers her? Hard to tell when the room was still spinning. "Psst...DJ. Hey, me, Brent. Wake up."

My God, it was like trying to wake the dead. Good thing he wasn't an ax murderer or anything. He just hoped that she'd appreciate his perseverance when she realized all he'd done to wake her. DJ groaned a little then rolled over to the opposite side of the bed. *Really*? Was he going to have to crawl in to get her? The thought did hold some appeal. He leaned over—God, it was a big bed. He'd heard of California king, but was there such a thing as a Texas king?—and jostled her shoulder. Well, that was what he meant to do, but he overestimated the distance, fell, and ended up face first eating mattress with his feet firmly planted on the floor.

Brent moaned. He was just so damn tired—coming up the stairs, finding DJ's room, half crawling into bed with her —all had been *soooooo* hard. He just needed a rest. Needed to gather his strength, get his story formulated in his brain. He just needed to close his eyes for a moment and figure out the best way to explain how he'd left her stinkin' drunk brother out in the middle of nowhere with only his cowboy boots and an empty whiskey bottle to keep him company.

———

"What in the hell are you doing in my *bed?*"

The noise. The noise was so loud. It was like the squeal

of tires on asphalt and nails on a chalkboard all rolled into one. Brent opened his eyes and did his cowboy-best to ignore the siren-red throb that had become his head. The sun was bright, not just bright, but a holy-white-light-of-God bright.

Please God, I promise to never drink again. Just let me not throw up.

He squinted his eyes and breathed through the nausea —this wasn't his first brush with a hangover—he could do this. He carefully turned his head to address the angry woman lying next to him. Strangely, this wasn't his first brush with an angry woman in his bed, either. Despite the red haze of the hangover and the cheery sunlight streaming through the window behind her, Brent could already make out she was pissed as hell.

So he did what he always did when he encountered a tight situation with really no easy way out—he threw his best smile.

It wasn't hard to do, DJ was beautiful. Even with her black-brown hair sticking out all around her head, her almond shaped eyes narrowed into black pools, and her juicy, full lips pressed into a thin line, he didn't have a hard time imagining what she'd look like smiling down at him. Probably the closest thing he'd ever get to an angel.

"I asked you a question, Rock Star, and I..." she paused, her nose wrinkling in disgust, then she carefully leaned in and took a cautionary sniff. Her eyes widened, and she clasped her hand to cover her mouth and nose. "Oh my God," her voice muffled from behind her palm, "you smell like cheap whiskey and rotting horse sh—."

A slight gagging sound broke off her last words. Of course, that was a pretty accurate description of what had happened last night. He watched her gaze flicker down his body and then widen in horror. Somehow he'd managed to pull himself up on the bed and find a nice fluffy pillow to rest his weary head on. He had sprawled out, taking more than his fair share of the bed, fully dressed, and on top of the covers. Thank God, he wasn't naked—there'd been a few minor incidents of streaking in his youth. No, it wasn't him being fully dressed that had steam rising from DJ's ears; it was what he'd forgotten to take off beforehand—his boots. The work boots had been an old pair Derrek had lying around, cracked and weather beaten, the soles were almost worn through, but that wasn't the only reason for DJ's fowl looks. Dark brown mud and horse manure was smeared in a wide arc across the foot of the bed. Bits of grass and a few large mud clomps decorated the girly white coverlet.

Slowly he scooted his boots off the side, spreading more creek bottom along the way. He searched his mind for an eloquent way of apologizing, but the words got stuck as she rose one perfectly arched bare foot to the middle of his stomach and pushed.

He landed on his back with a resounding thud followed by a loud grunt as all the air left his lungs. It hurt. Everything hurt. Maybe he could just stay here on her floor until he recovered. Maybe if he moaned really loud she'd take pity on him and leave him alone. He dared a glance. DJ loomed above from the side of her bed, and from the expression on her face his reprieve didn't seem likely.

That's when the yelling began. There were words. A long list of cleverly strung together names that all had generally the same meaning—dumbass. Then there was the dozen different ways she questioned his intelligence—what the hell were you thinking? Are you an idiot? How could you be so stupid?

Brent laid there and let the sharp hum of her words

wash over him. Really, other than sorry, there wasn't much he could say. He could only agree with her on every count, and really, was there even a defense for stupid? But he'd been around long enough to know the best way to deal with an angry woman was to let her vent. When DJ finally slowed down enough to draw a breath, she asked one question he had a hope of answering. "What do you have to say for yourself?"

Damn, he felt like he was twelve again. Did he have something to say for himself? He'd actually laid there and tried to come up with a well thought out excuse, except his attention got caught at how her thin shirt gapped as she leaned over, and he could see the beginning swell of her breasts. How the morning light streaming in from behind made her shirt partly transparent letting him see way more than he had the right to see. "Um...I..."

Damn, he had nothing.

No surprise that his answers weren't satisfying. Her midnight eyes glowed like liquid fire. They seemed darker than normal this morning. Fascinating, he wondered what color they'd change to if she ever allowed him near enough to kiss her again. "Don't you have anything to say? I mean, what are you thinking right now?"

Brent knew he had charm in spades, and he was just drunk enough to think he could still use this situation to his advantage. He propped himself up on one elbow, ignoring how the room spun, and smiled. "You want to know the truth?"

She nodded. Women always thought they wanted to know the truth, but really they wanted a prettied-up version of the truth.

"The truth is my biggest regret is that I spent my first night in your bed without remembering any of it." He ended with his sexy smile that he was pretty sure had landed him his music deal.

The look on her face was priceless, and it was even more priceless when she hopped out of bed and started kicking him with her barefoot toward the door. "Get the hell out of my room! I swear, if I see you anywhere near me for the rest of your stay, I'll get my daddy's shotgun and I will *not* hesitate to use it."

Brent started rolling toward the door. He knew when he wasn't welcome.

"Derrek!" DJ started to yell. The shriek was like knitting needles in his ears. "Derrek, get in here and get your loser, no good, nasty-smelling, ego-sucking friend out of my room before I do something I'll go to jail for later."

An image jostled loose inside Brent's brain. *Derrek! Oh crap.*

Brent jumped to his feet and grabbed the door frame for balance. "Wait, there's something I need to tell you."

She shook her head as she stood in front of him, arms crossed, legs bare and long in a pair of men's boxer shorts. The image was sexy as hell, and if she noticed how turned on he was right now he'd be sure to be picking buckshot out of his behind later.

"I don't want to hear anything you have to say," she yelled at him then turned her head to yell down the hallway. "Derrek, get in here and deal with your guest."

He held up his hand. "No, really. It's about Derrek."

That stopped her cold. "What about my brother? What in the hell have you done with my brother?"

A tickling of guilt started deep inside his belly. "Yeah, see, that's why I was in your room last night. I was coming to ask for your help."

Her smoky eyes widened. Yep, they were definitely

black. Good thing they weren't lasers or he'd be dead by now. "Help with what? How?"

He rose up a finger to give himself a moment. Last night was incredibly hazy. "To the best of my recollection, I think Derrek fell off his horse somewhere between the creek and the ranch, and I'm really hoping he didn't break his neck in the process."

TEN

She was going to kill Derrek. No, she was going to kill Brent, and then Derrek. Kill them both, because really, at their age, she shouldn't have to be dealing with this crap. She turned, grabbed her jersey jacket off the back of her chair, and ran down the stairs with Brent right behind her. She flung open the back door and jammed her bare feet into her boots while grabbing the keys off the rack. By the time they'd made it to her truck and driven some distance along the dirt road towards the creek, DJ's anger had turned into deep concern. If Derrek died because of some drunken, harebrained stunt and left her all alone in this world, she'd never forgive him.

DJ knew all too well that tragedies happened. She was no longer under the illusion that she and all that belonged to her were untouchable. Life happened, she got that, but she just didn't think she could go on living without her brother. Brent sat beside her; quiet, for once. Smart. If he said anything, she'd likely bite his head off.

All this was his fault. Even when Derrek and Brent had

been kids, they'd always gotten into trouble. Derrek was the most steadfast guy that she knew, until Brent came around. Then it seemed like all his sense was thrown out the window. That first summer after their parents died had been the roughest. Derrek was barely eighteen, and DJ was only fifteen. More than anything, she needed the stable environment that her parents had always provided for her—the ranch, the house, school. With so much upheaval, DJ depended on Derrek's routines, but all that seemed to come to a crashing halt whenever Brent called. Neither one of them would hear from Brent for months at a time while he was playing gigs in some back-water, two-bit town, and then, out of the blue, Brent would call and Derrek would head for the hills. Derrek would be gone for a whole weekend, one time a full-on week, and DJ's life had crumbled.

She couldn't blame either one of them. They'd both been young, stupid, and too good-looking for their own good. Derrek had always taken his responsibilities seriously, both to her and to the ranch. It was just that every time DJ woke to an empty house she felt the loss of her parents that much more. She was older now, she didn't need someone to babysit her or make sure she ate her dinner, but it was still hard not to be resentful of all the time Derrek had spent with Brent.

Brent's hand reached over and squeezed hers, pulling her out of the past. She resisted the instinctual urge to sock him one. "I'm sorry, DJ," Brent said. "I didn't mean for any of this to happen. I know you're worried."

"I'm not worried." She removed her hand from his grasp and placed it on the steering wheel. Touching Brent was confusing: comforting and exciting at the same time.

"I can hear your teeth grinding from here." If he noticed

her brush off, he didn't seem too bothered. The man's skin was thicker than a warthog's. "You're worried, and I get it. If I were you, I would be, too, but Derrek's a grown man. He'll be fine once he sleeps off the whiskey."

She glanced at Brent and immediately regretted it. Damn, even hung over, hair uncombed, shirt sweaty and nasty, he still looked good. Like rough-hot-dirty-bad-boy good. She wasn't even sure exactly what that meant, but if it had been anyone *but* Brent she wouldn't be opposed to finding out.

"I can't believe you left him out there." Glad they were going slow since she couldn't seem to take her eyes off him. "What were you thinking?"

To his credit, he winced. "I thought we established that... I hadn't been thinking. I'd been *drrriiiiinking*. Those two things are mutually exclusive. And really, I didn't mean to leave him. I was going to grab you for help and then... then..."

"You fell asleep." Were all men this irritating, or was it just him?

He raised both hands up as if to ward off another argument. "In my defense, I don't remember falling asleep, and I'm sure I tried to wake you several times."

DJ pierced him with a look. "Are you really trying to blame this on me?"

"Is there any chance at all it will work?"

"None."

"Then absolutely not," he said, shaking his head and throwing his hands up in surrender.

DJ rolled her eyes heavenward. If he was ugly it would be so much easier to throw him from her truck and not feel bad about it. "Not everything is a joke, you know?"

Brent groaned and slouched down in the front seat. "I know, please, I'm sorry. Can we not-" Brent sat back up and pointed over her left shoulder. "Hey look, there's our guy."

DJ followed his point and suppressed a sigh of relief at the sight of a bedraggled cowboy limping along the dirt road, an arm cradling his ribs, head down and low against the brilliant Texas sun. DJ smiled. He must have one hell of a headache.

They pulled up alongside him, and Brent scooted over to the middle while Derrek gingerly sat himself by the passenger door with a loud groan.

"Hard night?" Okay, she just couldn't resist. It was a sister's prerogative. It didn't help any that the stench inside the cab had just doubled.

"Jesus, Mary, and Joseph, I'm gonna die," Derrek muttered, his face already two shades paler than normal.

"You throw up in my truck, and I swear to God I'll throw you out and make you walk. I swear I will." Now that she knew her brother was okay, good old-fashioned irritation raised its head. Sisterly affection could only be pushed so far, and cleaning puke up after her brother's hard night of drinking was where she drew the line.

Derrek nodded, and then rolled down the window and stuck his head out, but DJ noticed that with each inhale he winced. "Are you okay?"

He nodded. "I think I broke a few ribs. I just need to get home and get into the shower. I'll be fine."

DJ groaned. "Do you seriously think you broke your ribs?"

Derrek didn't say anything, but by the look on his face she could tell that was a yes.

"I'm taking you to the ER." *Perfect*. Just what she needed, but a visceral level of concern had her gripping the steering wheel as she made her way out to the main road.

She glanced over at her brother and took in his grayed-out expression. The morning was already getting late, and she still had to check the feed before it was delivered to the horses, then get them exercised. Though she had good men working for her, it was hard to let go of even the smallest things concerning the ranch. Derrek said that habit was going to kill her. Right now, it seemed more like familial ties would do the trick. "How the hell did you break a rib?"

Brent actually snorted beside her. Did he think any of this was funny? When was this man going to be leaving her house?

"He fell off his horse," he said, with more humor in his voice than the situation warranted.

"You're a jerk, Brent." Derrek said, taking a break from the head out the window position, but staying close just in case. "Officially, the horse got spooked and kicked me, but I don't suppose you're ever going to let me live this one down."

"A cowboy who falls off his horse. Total embarrassment to everything Texas. How you can even hold your head up, I don't know," Brent said, but when DJ glanced at him she noticed that Brent had started to look a bit green around the edges.

"I can't, if you haven't already noticed," Derrek said, going back to his head-out-the-window pose. "No thanks to you."

DJ had had enough. If Derrek was able to hold his own with Brent then he was going to live. Besides, once those two got started there'd be nothing but bickering from here on out, and frankly, she wasn't in the mood. "Right, and crawling into the wrong bed is any better?"

That brought Derrek's color back better than any bucket of ice water in the face could. "Whose bed?"

There was just the low whirl of the AC and the hum of the motor as DJ pulled out on to the main road.

Derrek didn't let it drop. "Whose bed? You said he crawled into the wrong bed last night, so whose bed?"

God, this was awkward. DJ sighed. "Mine, but it sounds worse than it is. Nothing happened. He basically got confused and then passed out." She couldn't believe she was defending Brent. What was wrong with her?

She wasn't sure what she expected from Derrek—righteous indignation, protectiveness, brotherly outrage. Instead, he snorted, since laughing probably hurt too bad.

She looked over at him. Derrek shrugged with a half-hearted smile. "No, sorry sis, it isn't funny. I'm just so relieved that it wasn't my bed. I saw the crap he rolled in last night, and I just couldn't stand the thought of him in my sheets."

There was another bark of laughter from Brent. "Bro, you should've seen her face when she woke up and saw that I still had my boots on. I thought she was going to crap bricks she was so mad."

Both men fell into a fit of adolescent laughter.

DJ made the right turn a bit too sharp, which had one man groaning and the other clamping his palm over his mouth. She'd been woken by an uninvited man in her bed, had been forced to run out the door in nothing but her pj's and a sweater, and had to drive to the ER like she had nothing better to do. For the love of everything reasonable, she hadn't even had her coffee this morning. Anger crawled up her throat. The ER loomed on the right. She turned the wheel and pulled up in front of the entrance. Apparently even that was too much for them, since both men groaned out loud. She turned and glared at them both. "Get out!"

Both men looked at her. All traces of humor were gone.

Brent mumbled something under his breath, but Derrek seemed the one most confused.

"It's not going to get any easier the longer you wait," she said. "Out. Now."

Derrek's sad eyes came out in full. He did look rather pathetic. "Can I call you to come get me when I'm done?"

Brent piped up in a weak voice between them, "Umm... yeah...uh, I need to get out."

DJ didn't spare him a glance. All her focus was on her brother. "Nope."

"Really?" Derrek whined.

"Dude, I need to get out," Brent said a bit more loudly.

"Nope." DJ shook her head, loving how the tables had turned. "If you can give me a hard time then I'm sure you're gonna live."

"Dude. NOW!"

Both siblings turned their attention toward Brent. And then two things happened at once: Derrek finally started to move his butt, and DJ started yelling. "Swallow it, Brent! You better swallow it! So help me God, you throw up in my truck I'm gonna..."

It was too late. Derrek got out in time to avoid collateral damage, but DJ's dash took the full brunt.

After that, a heavy silence filled the air along with the thick stench of vomit.

Brent took the tail of his shirt and wiped at his mouth, DJ focused straight ahead, trying not to let the tears of anger fill her eyes, while Derrek slowly started to back away from them both.

"I should go put my name in," Derrek said, a thumb

pointing behind him towards the entrance as he shuffled backwards. "You never know how long the wait's gonna be. So...I...

And then he was gone, moving through the automatic ER doors faster than any man with a broken rib should have.

ELEVEN

*T*he sun beat down on Brent like the iron fist of God as he walked along the side of the road trying his damnedest not to get hit by passing traffic. After puking in DJ's truck, apologizing profusely, and promising to clean the mess up, he'd pretty much chickened out of any more conversation with her and ran inside the hospital after Derrek. When he'd gone into the waiting room to give moral support to his best friend, Derrek just shook his head and pointed toward the seats in the opposite corner. "Don't even think about it, bro. Don't even come near me."

It wasn't long before the other patients started to murmur and cover their noses. He knew when a crowd had turned against him. It wasn't the first time he'd had to make a speedy exit. With few options left, Brent decided that walking off his hangover wasn't the worst thing he could do. Except he'd forgotten how far the Double D Ranch was and how freaking *hot* it was for June.

Just then a truck zoomed by. The bass thumping, windows down, and some punk kid threw an empty beer can at Brent, barely missing his head. "Get a job, you bum!"

Brent didn't say a word. Just shook his head and groaned. From rock star to bum in less than a week. *Stellar, dude. Stellar.*

The mile and a half walk back helped clear his head, and had him sweating out the last of the fireball whiskey. By the time he'd stumbled into the bunkhouse his shirt was soaked through, his head pounding, and he was in dire need of some coffee.

Yes, he needed to go and grovel at DJ's feet, but that was going to have to wait until after he had time to make himself feel human again. He stripped off his clothes on his way to the bathroom and jumped in the shower while the water was still cold.

Lord, couldn't DJ have picked a better time to leave him stranded then during the middle of a heat wave? He stepped out of the shower and donned some clothes. He checked his phone to see what time it was. It was after eight in the morning. Late enough that he was pretty sure he wouldn't encounter anyone in the kitchen. He had no desire to set eyes on DJ, at least not right now. He knew he'd have to apologize again, but he just wasn't up for the sharp side of her tongue or that condescending arch of her eyebrow that literally took him from zero to ten on the pissed-off scale in five seconds flat.

The darkened kitchen was a welcome contrast to the overly bright, overly hot day outside, and Brent immediately appreciated the quiet stillness of an empty house. The left over scents of bacon and eggs still lingered, but the thought of food turned his stomach rather than making his mouth water.

He started to open and close cabinet doors trying to find where DJ stashed the medicine. He knew exactly what he needed: Alka-Seltzer, two aspirins, coffee, and bed. He was never going to drink again. Never. Scout's honor and all the other empty promises that came with the morning after. Really, he was too old for this crap.

The back door opened and shut, and by the tapping of quick steps, Brent knew his reprieve was over. He drew in a quick breath and relaxed his body into his calm, devil-may-care stance. There was no way in hell he'd let her see how much he was suffering. DJ was like a she-lion on the hunt. She'd sense his weakness and then eat him for breakfast.

DJ strolled into the kitchen head high, shoulders back, confidence exuded like the scent of perfume. She tossed her hat on the table and began to pull off her leather work gloves. She looked as hot as he'd been walking back from the hospital. Sweat trailed clean streaks down the side of her dusty cheeks, hair wet and slightly matted in a messy pony-tail, gray tank top darkened with moisture. The cut-off jean shorts with brown cowboy boots just completed the look of a hard working rancher.

She looked up at him, the hard glint of her almond eyes already making his gut tighten. "Good afternoon, *Rock Star*." she said, condescension crammed full into each word like an overstuffed carry-on.

"Howdy, *Rancher*," he said, doing a little nickname cramming of his own.

"So you're up? I really didn't expect to see hide nor hair of you today." One hand rested on her hip, and not for the first time, he noticed how awesome her arms were. There was something about her well-defined shoulders, a cotton tank top clinging to wet skin, and then those damn short-jean shorts that proved her legs were just as sexy as the rest of her.

Maybe it was because she looked capable, not willowy and fragile like the super models he dated. Maybe it was because he liked strong women who didn't let him get away with anything. Or maybe... maybe it was because with her hair disheveled, skin all golden-brown and glistening, and her chest rapidly moving up and down like she was pissed off or recovering from strenuous activity, she looked exactly how he wanted her to look after spending a night in his bed.

He finally realized his mistake. While he'd been staring the whole time, thinking of DJ and bed, and his bed with DJ in it, she'd been waiting for an answer.

"A little slow on the uptake this morning?" She punctuated her words with a slap of her glove on the table. Dust motes danced like pixies in the sunlight, reminding him of the fairy in the story of Peter Pan, the boy who never wanted to grow up—how apropos. "So, how are you feeling this bright and cheery morning?"

Awful. "Great," he said, not feeling at all guilty about the lie.

"Oh really?" Her brows furrowed, and her lush mouth did that old-lady puckered look that turned him on and pissed him off at the same time. "Not too tired? Your little upset stomach is all gone?"

He was literally dying on the spot, but he shrugged one shoulder, all casual-like. "Nope, good as new."

"Oh," she tilted her head to the side, her voice reaching a sickly sweet octave. "Great. Then you wouldn't mind mucking out the stalls again this morning, seeing that I got off to a late start and all."

He leaned against the counter, hoping to look totally at ease instead of dizzy as hell. "Oh yeah, I would love to, except..." Finally his brain kicked in enough to come up with an excuse. He snapped his fingers, loving how her jaw tightened at the sound. "I gotta pick up Derrek. I'm sure he's ready by now."

"Really?" She smiled a smile that told him she didn't buy a word he said.

"Really." He threw a smile back that said *take this crap I'm feeding you and eat it.*

She blew a loud *tsk* sound from behind her teeth. "Figures."

There were a few words in a woman's language that got under his skin—*fine, nothing, whatever you say,* and, of course, *figures.* Brent had been around women long enough to know what *figures* meant. He knew it was a female's way of saying he was a complete jackass, but she was the only person in the room smart enough to realize it.

He wasn't going to fight with her. He was an adult. He knew how to defuse situations. He was going to walk away and... "Really? And what exactly is that supposed to mean?"

She tossed a few misplaced hairs out of her eyes and tightened her jaw. Apparently, she was also up for a fight. Might've been something to do with him puking in her truck. "It means that's all I'd expect from a person like you. Your idea of a full day's work is to stare out the window and think up some overdone love song."

Okay, that pissed him off. DJ could think whatever she wanted about him personally. He even didn't mind the "I'm-so-much-better-than-you-because-I-have-a-horse-ranch" attitude, but he was sick of her digs at him professionally. She didn't have to respect his music, but she needed to respect the hard work he'd put into his career. He pushed himself away from the counter and stood straight, anger getting his blood pumping. "You, DJ," he nodded his chin in her direction and then took a sip of coffee. "You know what you sound like?"

"What?" Her brows arched questioningly, her body braced with arms-crossed and closed off.

"A hater. Man, you hate the fact that I make a damn good living doing what I love. I think you're jealous."

Her chin went up a notch, and he could tell she was biting the inside of her lip, probably to keep from telling him off. The "Ha!" was forced, but she tried to pass it off as a laugh. "Jealous of you? No, Brent, I'm not. In fact, you are the exact opposite of what I'd be jealous of."

Man, he wanted to wipe that smug smile off her face so bad. He so wanted to get under her skin; make her lose her cool. He set his coffee cup down and made his way from behind the counter. "Wow, you know, I finally figured it out. I know what your problem is."

"Oh, please tell me. I love getting advice from a man who's never had a relationship last longer than two weeks and who breaks out into a cold sweat at the thought of a hard day's work." She tossed her hair behind her shoulder with the same animosity as she flung her words.

He stalked her, moving closer to his prey. Only the kitchen table separated them, and yet, even that seemed too much distance. "You know what your problem is? You're too uptight. You need to get laid."

She gasped.

Yeah, he'd never actually told a woman that before, but he couldn't back down now. "And I mean *bad*. I thought I needed some action, but girl, you make my itch seem like a mosquito bite."

There was a moment of stunned silence on her part, and he had to admit it was nice to see her at a loss for words. But that moment didn't last long. "So to continue your analogy, that would make my itch...?

He smiled. "Like poison oak."

She stepped away, as if needing to put distance between them. He watched her walk back and forth behind the table, hands on her hips, back straight, chest out. Damn, she had nice looking breasts.

She turned to face him, her eyes narrowing, full lips in a half smile. "And I'm sure you know just the person who could... scratch my itch?"

Hell yeah, he did, and maybe if they could stop fighting and start screwing, he could finally write some more songs. "It's real simple, Sugar. You scratch my itch, and I would definitely love to scratch yours."

DJ took a moment. He watched emotions fleet across her eyes like a fast-moving storm, and when pissed off and anger was finally replaced by hurt, all Brent's previous humor left. He took a breath. He didn't want to hurt DJ, and the thought that he did something to cause her pain— pissing her off was okay— but to cause tears to well up in her eyes crushed him.

"Sorry, Brent," she said. "I never make the same mistake twice."

And there it was. Really, he knew it all along. The whole reason for her hostility and her attitude. It came down to some poorly timed kiss when they'd both been kids. Brent rubbed at his forehead, a sharp pain building behind his eyes. The one in his heart was worse. "DJ, I can't even begin to tell how sor-"

"Were we not friends?" She didn't let him finish. Why should she? His apology was ten years too late. "Did that kiss not mean anything to you?"

How the hell had he gone from wanting to fight with her to wanting to take her in his arms and tell her everything was going to be okay? He hadn't known that she had the ability to play his emotions so well. But instead of saying all that, or doing what his heart told him, he stood his ground and waited.

DJ pulled out a chair. She didn't just sit, but collapsed as if she couldn't remain standing under her own strength. He followed suit, for some reason not wanting to loom over her anymore. She looked out the window, the sunlight choosing at that moment to break through a cloud, throwing sun beams at the whips of her hair that floated around her face.

He fisted his hands and brought them to his forehead at a loss for the right words. When he'd given her that kiss, he'd been eighteen and an idiot. He hadn't known jack back then. And he sure the hell hadn't taken a fifteen-year-old girl's heart into consideration. "I was a stupid kid. Please don't hold the actions of a teenager against me now."

A halfhearted shrug competed with her sad smile. "And what about the one the other day? You're not eighteen anymore. Did that not mean anything either? What's your excuse this time?"

"I don't. I don't..." He let his voice dissipate like the thin wisp of smoke from a forgotten cigarette

He'd never been good at these types of things. That was why he'd always gone for the easy girl who never expected more from him. If he kept their expectations low then they were never disappointed. She looked at him, her dark almond eyes twin pools of emotion, and that's when he knew. He saw her pain, her heartbreak, and her disappointment in him. And he knew exactly what she was going to say next.

"Where were you?"

Oh, no. He shook his head. *No.*

"Where. Were. You?" She plopped out the words like each one was its own sentence.

He groaned and buried his face in his hands. No anything else but this, not this. He didn't want to go there. "Please, DJ, I don't want to do this."

"Don't do what? Don't talk about it? Why? Is it too painful for you, Brent? Too much?" Her voice rose, but it wasn't the sharp playful anger of before, but the deeper one of hidden hurt. "My parents died. Died that summer. Derrek and I were left all alone, and where were you? You left when we needed you the most. When... I needed you."

He closed his eyes; he couldn't look at her. The songs he had written at that time had been filled with lyrics about guilt and regret. Each ballad a poetry of self-hate and shame. It had taken him years to forgive himself for not coming back to Somewhere when Derrek had needed him most. That summer, while Derrek's life imploded, Brent's had taken off. He'd gotten his first offer for a real paying gig. At the time he'd thought it had been the real thing, but in reality it was just a spot on a tour as a minor backup singer for the next up-and-coming pop star. Brent thought it would be his ticket to fame, but of course, nothing was that easy.

After he'd come back from the tour, he'd called Derrek and basically begged his best friend's forgiveness for not showing up for the funeral. He'd barely made it through his apology, when Derrek, damn him, being such a freaking good guy, had simply told him he'd never held that against Brent, and if he hadn't taken that opportunity Derrek would've kicked him.

Derrek had forgiven him, which allowed Brent to finally forgive himself.

But apparently there'd been more apologies he'd needed to make.

Brent looked up at DJ. Where to start? At eighteen he hadn't been equipped to handle the fallout of Mr. and Mrs. Diaz's death. He'd been too rattled by his own emotions, much less able to help Derrek with his. So he'd avoided the whole situation, pretended that nothing had changed, nothing had happened. Very telling, that at twenty-seven, denial was still very much a part of his coping mechanism.

"I needed a friend too, you know," she swallowed. "You weren't just Derrek's friend. At least at the time, I thought we were friends also."

He didn't know what to say. He cared too much for her to lie. He'd known back then that he couldn't be the man that she needed. He knew it now. "I'm sorry."

Those were the lamest two words he'd ever spoke in his life. How did she reduce him to this with just a few words and a glance his way?

She shook her head. Her jaw tightened as he watched. He could feel the barrier she was constructing against him, and for some reason, that action pained him more than anything else. Her next words made the wall that much harder to scale.

"This ranch is my home. The place I wake up to every morning, what I pour my blood, sweat, and tears into. I've worked for everything my whole life, and depended on no one but myself. As sure as the sun rising tomorrow, this is where I'm going to live all my days, and if I have anything to say about it, where I'll take my last breath. This is my home, my heart, and my life. So if some man will be scratching my itch, it will be a man I can count on as much as I do myself."

Brent wanted to reach out and grab her hand, but he lost his nerve. "DJ, I want you to listen to me. Really, really, I'm so sorry for bailing that summer. I was young and stupid and totally unequipped for what that summer meant for all of us. It was the last of our innocence and Derrek, damn him, stepped up and took it like a man. I, on the other hand, have always fallen way short. I freaked out. Got scared. I didn't know what to do, but I want you to know if you ever need me like that again, I won't fail you. I promise. I'll be here for you."

DJ nodded and swiped at her eyes with the same irritation one would a pesky fly. He could tell she didn't cry often, and when she did it was never in front of others. "It was a long time ago. And I understand. Not sure what you could've done if you were here anyways. It sucked no matter how it all played out."

He wanted to wipe the sadness out of her eyes. Fix the hurt. He'd seen the same look in Derrek's face when they'd met up over the years, and to recognize it in DJ's broke his heart. The Diaz's needed a little fun in their lives. They needed a reason to smile and just enjoy the day for what it brought. Any emotion was better than the lonely desperation that they seemed to wear so well. "Thank you, and just so you know, my offer still stands."

She looked up, eyes still watery, but there was a smile on her face. "What?"

"You still need to get laid."

Her eyes widened and mouth dropped open, but her eyes danced and there was color in her cheeks. She didn't waste any time; she reached across the table, grabbed his coffee mug, and attempted to throw the contents in his face.

Attempted, because he was quicker than she and ducked. Coffee sloshed on the floor, after which he popped his head back up, confident she'd run out of ammunition.

"I can't believe you said that! Didn't you just hear my speech about a man I can count on?" She shook her head, but a smile danced where once her puckered look had been. "You are such a jerk."

He suppressed a laugh, looked down at the spilled coffee and then back at her. "And I can't believe you wasted that coffee. That was the last of it, you know. And I'm assuming you had your fair share, since there were only cold dregs left. What do you do, take it intravenously?"

She rolled her eyes. He was used to that exasperated look on the ladies, but for some reason on DJ it made him happy. "I can't believe that after everything I told you,"—she checked the coffee cup, seemingly annoyed that it was empty— "that you are still trying to get into my pants."

Well, she hadn't said no. He could work with exasperated. Exasperated was halfway home. It was all in the presentation.

Point one: Always acknowledge that you've heard everything a woman has been saying.

"Okay," he held up his hands in mock surrender. "I've heard everything you said."

Point two: Always agree with a woman, even if you don't. Agreeing doesn't mean she's right, just that you don't want to argue with her.

"And I totally agree the Marlboro man of the west is exactly the type of man you need."

Point three: Women LOVED to listen to a man, especially when he's specifically asked her to listen to him. "But here's my proposal. All I ask is that you wait until I'm done presenting my case before making a decision."

And getting them to hold off on their decision just meant he kept talking until they were convinced.

DJ crossed her arms, causing her breasts to strain the boundary of what her tank top could hold. The lush mounds almost spilled over—holy hell, he was going to have to write a song about those—he looked away for a brief second to keep focused. He knew DJ barely wore any make up, so he'd bet his favorite guitar that they were real. He'd lived in L.A. for the past few years, so he'd almost forgotten what real *felt* like. He'd love to get reacquainted.

"You've a captive audience, something I think you're all too comfortable with." Her gaze narrowed, but there was no more sadness, and he knew he'd lay down on a railroad track to keep her tears away.

He licked his lips, swallowed, and then made a show of cracking his knuckles. He was a showman to the bone.

She laughed. He decided right then and there that if one day he could capture that sound with his music, he'd die a happy man. "I've been around both you and Derrek for some time, so I feel I'm in a position to make a few observations."

She nodded. "Observe away."

"You both work too hard. I see it in your face. Derrek, being a guy, can handle a few wrinkles, but Sugar, at twenty-four you're already getting creases in your forehead."

She gasped and slapped her hand over her forehead. "I'm getting wrinkles? Oh my God. I... I..."

The total panic in her face had him scrambling to cover his remark. "Now wait a minute, don't freak out. This is what I'm telling you. I've got a cure for that and for a lot of other aliments you're suffering from. I-"

That brought her no comfort. Panic riddled her features. "Are there other wrinkles? I know my mom turned gray at thirty, but I thought I still had a few more years..."

Oh man, what can of worms had he opened? He'd never get anywhere if he didn't cut this line of conversation off.

"Hey," he got her attention with a palm slap to the table. "You only get the privilege of interrupting me if we're sleeping together. And since we're not..." He raised both eyebrows, allowing her time to fill in the blank.

She got the point. "Continue," she said, a circling motion with her hand.

"Having fun can help you with all that. Fun is good. Fun

is okay. Fun makes people happy." He emphasized his words with a wide smile.

She didn't look convinced.

"Here, say it with me," he tried again. "Fffffuuuuunnnn."

"Fun," she deadpanned.

He groaned. "Good God, you even say it boring. I've never met anyone who says that word with less enthusiasm. That's it. You need a fun intervention, which is where I come in."

She tried to fight it, but her lips quivered with the need to smile, and her exotic upturned eyes danced back at him. "And I suppose you have experience with this sort of intervention," she said with all seriousness.

He loved that she was playing along. If only he could make her laugh again, his whole hangover experience would be worth it. He stood up, braced his palms on the table, and leaned in closer to her. "Oh honey, trust me, I'm the best man for this job."

She arched a brow. "Your cockiness should be annoying."

He nodded knowingly. "I know, I ride that fine line between annoying and endearing."

She stifled a chuckle. The sound sent chills down his spine and his heart thumping like he was playing in front of a sold-out stadium. "Okay, so here are my three points. I figure a good solid three arguments could convince just about anyone. So if I prove that having sex with me is a once-in-a-lifetime experience, you'll have to at least think about it. Deal?"

Her head tilted to the side. "I'm afraid to interrupt you at this point."

"Good enough. Point number one." He put one finger

up. "Sex feels good. Sex with me will make your skin glow all warm and tingly and your breath all quick and fast."

She shook her head. "I can get that from a really good three mile run."

"Two." Second finger went up. "Having sex with me will cause that half-excitement half-adrenaline rush that spreads throughout your body, which some have described as an actual out-of-body experience."

She nodded, lips in an old-lady pucker, which strangely was fast becoming one of the most erotic gestures he'd ever seen. "You just described the exact feeling I get when I try a new jump with my horse. That's it perfectly."

Okay, he was a big boy, he could handle being shot down. He nodded, conceding the point to her. This was his last big moment and he had to play it perfectly. "Come here." He used his finger to beckon her closer.

She shook her head. "What? Why? I can hear you from here."

Not way over there with her arms crossed like some kinda closed off genie. "I need you closer for this one. It's really important, and I want to make sure you get the full sense of it."

Was he surprised when she stood up and placed her hands on the table? Maybe a little bit, but whatever, his hopes just soared.

They were a few inches apart, fingers touching, bodies leaning in, each closing a little less than half of the table width. He could smell her scent of soap and honeysuckle, of leather and hard work, and suddenly the mix was the most intoxicating aroma he'd ever taken in.

"Closer," he said, his voice a rough whisper, which wasn't at all an act. He found he was having a hard time keeping his cool, especially with the tightening of his jeans making him uncomfortable.

She looked up at him from under her hooded lashes, then pushed out her lower lip slightly.

He licked his own and swallowed.

She leaned forward, almost causing their lips to touch. There was a part of his brain that told him she was teasing the hell out of him, but another large part of his anatomy that said he didn't care.

"Is this close enough?" Her voice was a mere whisper. He felt every word against his lips, could hear every inhale of breath. His wasn't the only heart rate that was elevated.

"Point four."

"You said there were only three points."

He didn't miss a beat. "Point three and a half, having sex with me guarantees you the best orgasm of your life. And if that isn't F.U.N., I don't know what is."

Her eyes narrowed and the tiniest furrow in her brow appeared. "And how would one guarantee that? Because I have a vibrator with the exact same wording on the back of the box."

Oh, she was a funny one. "Oh, Sugar, if you're comparing me to a vibrator then I'm definitely a shoo-in for the best of your life, no question."

Her eyes went sexy dark, and then broke his gaze to look down at his mouth. She moved in a bit closer so that their lips were touching, but just barely. And then she stopped. No further, just the lightest of touches.

It was the sexiest move he'd ever seen. It took everything in him not to grab her face with his palms and kiss her right then and there.

"Well..." her lips brushed against his, "you've given me a

lot to think about. Her voice was sexy rough like sand over velvet and it was hot as hell. "But..."

Oh dear lord, there was a "but..."

"But I had a late start this morning, and I've got to get back to work."

And with that she pulled away, rounded the table, and started back toward the door.

Oh no, no way. She couldn't leave him hanging like that. "DJ, so is that a yes?"

She turned, and damn if she didn't have that I-know-exactly-what-I-did smirk on her face. "You're the rock star... figure it out."

TWELVE

*D*J made her way out of the kitchen, out the back door, and over to the side of the stables with her head high and her steps sure and steady.

And then she lost it.

Crap. She leaned against the wood paneling of the barn, wrapped her arms around her stomach, and tapped her head against the wall.

What had just happened? Had she really just spent a whole hour flirting with Brent Kane, one of country music's most sought after bachelors, and its most notorious woman-izer? Her lips still tingled where they'd met with Brent's. She touched her fingers to her mouth, noticed herself trembling, then got pissed off and shoved her hands into the pockets of her jean cut-offs.

She glanced around to make sure there were no eye-witnesses to her complete weak-kneed moment. She'd spent years gaining the respect of her crew. Most ranch hands came with the preconceived notion that a woman couldn't run a successful ranch and that it was beneath them to take orders from a female boss. She fought their chauvinism by being a tough as nails, no nonsense boss, who did her best to treat everyone fairly. The last thing she needed was for one of them to see her flustered over a pretend kiss and some flirtation.

DJ made her way into the cooler shade of the stables and, out of habit, added to the running check list in her mind of all the things she needed to do. The ranch was quiet for this time of day. It was one of those rare occurrences when things seemed to be going smoothly and they'd gotten on top of most of the chores. She sauntered up to the far stall and made kissing noises to the mare inside. The old quarter horse lifted her head and trotted over to her owner. DJ rubbed Queenie's rough nose between her hands and immediately felt a sense of calm steal over her. The coppery-red sorrel had been the first horse DJ's parent's had bought for her, and now, even though Queenie was too old to be much use around the ranch, DJ had never considered getting rid of her. The tired brown eyes looked up at DJ as if begging for a treat. With her pockets empty, DJ sighed and scratched between Queenie's ears instead. Was this enough? Were her ranch and horses enough? Or was there something more?

Every moment of every day had always been about her ranch, her horses. She told herself that she couldn't afford to flirt or spend prime daylight hours talking about F.U.N with some blond, too-handsome-for-his-own-good superstar just because she'd caught his interest for a hot second.

But still, something that Brent had said resonated with her. It was the same thing that Derrek would ride her about. She was too young to work herself into the grave. She saw a flash of what her life would look like in thirty years. She'd be all alone and old, waking up to realize that life had passed her by and all she had to show for it was some great horses and a dusty old ranch. Maybe she did need to have fun and live a little. God, would it really be so bad to have super-hot sex with a rock star? With Brent?

The logical, sane part of her was firmly in the "It's-a-bad-idea" camp, while a small part of her was on its knees, begging, "*Please, please, please* just this once say yes."

It was a temptation, alright. What was there not to like? Scruffy blond hair that brushed his collar and desperately needed a trim, well-toned body, dreamy blue eyes, and a charming, boyish smile that caused her insides to melt.

You and a thousand other women, sista'.

That was what she had to keep in mind. She knew how a fling with Brent would end. She'd been heart-broken and disappointed by him before. She wasn't special to Brent; never would be, never had been.

Soon after realizing that DJ had nothing special to give her, Queenie grew bored and went back to her bucket of oats. With no pressing chore to keep herself distracted, DJ rested her arms on the smooth, painted wood of the stall door and let her mind wander. She still remembered sitting in her bedroom after her parent's funeral, staring out the window, hoping and praying that Brent was on his way.

At the time she hadn't really believed her parents were dead. Sure, she'd heard the town's people whispering —*shock, grief, denial.* Maybe it had been strange that she hadn't cried over her parents' deaths since the night Derrek had opened their front door and a police officer stood on the wood porch. The blue and red lights from his squad car circled behind him, the sirens switched to silence as if to notify the world there was no need to hurry.

But she'd still believed that Brent's coming would make everything better. She imagined him waltzing through her door in a pair of blue jeans and that special smile she liked to believe he reserved just for her. He wouldn't patronize her with limp hugs and wet cheek kisses or a small, sad smile and a look of pity on his face. No, he'd blow in like a whirlwind, like a stiff breeze from the north, and pick her up in a bear hug, squeezing her tight until her ribs hurt.

And when he showed up, she wouldn't care that he'd gone off to Nashville to make it big and live his dream. She wouldn't even be angry anymore that he'd left her. Left her and hadn't even shown up for her parents' funeral.

She'd been willing to forgive him for not being there when she needed him the most—the part when they'd lowered matching coffins into the ground, her mom and dad side by side in the soft earth, together in death like they had been in life. It hadn't even mattered that the day mocked her with its brilliant blue sky and cheery sun. With its gentle breeze that had flirted with her black skirt and tried to play keep-away with the ponytail holder in her hair. Or that what she really had wanted was for it to rain. Rain and storm and crash with lightning so fierce that it shook the earth, because when Brent did come, he'd chase the non-existent clouds away and bring in his own kind of sunshine. He'd make the horrible day better. Even if just for a moment, even if just for the tiny expanse of time when she was in his arms, his clean scent filling her nose, her breath catching in her lungs, things would be better with Brent there.

So she had sat and waited that day. Waited until the porch lights turned on, cars drove back down the drive, the moon replaced the taunting sun, and night overtook the uncaring blue sky.

But Brent had never come. DJ learned a hard lesson that day—she wasn't important to Brent. Music was what he lived for, and no one, especially her, was more important than that.

DJ lay in bed and waited for her alarm to go off. It was four thirty in the morning, the sun wasn't even up, and though she'd never been so tired in her life, she knew from experience that she wouldn't be able to go back to sleep. Sleepless nights, early mornings, and a low level of irritation trailed her like a black cloud. Her body ached from the long days she'd been putting in. She would've liked to blame her sleeplessness solely on her brother's injury preventing him from working on the ranch, but if she was honest it had been like this ever since Brent had come into town.

She would've been okay if Brent's stay had lasted the original long weekend, but after Derrek had gotten home from the hospital, he'd been all too happy to inform her that Brent had prolonged his visit so he could help DJ with the extra workload. Derrek, stupid man, had no idea why having Brent around only made things worse for her, not better. Her work suffered—not because Brent didn't help around the ranch, surprisingly, he had— but because she'd been distracted. She had almost gotten a chunk taken out of her arm the other day because she'd been sneaking a peek of Brent shirtless in jeans and an old pair of cowboy boots as he'd given a horse a bath.

She didn't remember him being as tanned as he was, or as muscular. The tats were also new. She wondered if he went around shirtless just to annoy her. It worked. The fantasies of him, his white, million dollar smile, and the way he could make her laugh even when there was nothing remotely funny about what he said all contributed to her unease. No matter how much she tried to avoid or ignore him, he seemed always to be there. That was, until the evenings, when he sequestered himself in his room and strummed on his guitar till all hours of the morning.

One good thing did come from Brent being around. DJ realized that she did need to get a life. All work and no play made DJ a dull girl. She was going to go back to that book club, and there was nothing wrong with hanging out at Everyday Joe's on Friday and Saturday nights. She was young, she needed to live, and find someone who would like to slow dance with her.

Slow dance to one of Brent's songs?

The thought made her uncomfortable. Maybe she should start listening to jazz.

She still had a half an hour before her alarm went off, but decided she might as well get up. The thought of spending another day drooling over Brent was enough incentive for her to get up and get started. Maybe she'd be able to cut out early and run into town for a badly needed haircut and pedicure.

She slammed her fist into the pillow beside her. Really? A freaking pedicure? When had she ever cared about what color her toes were painted? But she knew the answer. Since drop-dead gorgeous Brent Kane had started teasing her about how good a little F-U-N with him would be. Something happened when he looked at her like that—teased her and told her how desirable she was—she believed him.

That damn shaggy hair, stunning blue eyes, even the dark green of the tat on his right shoulder and the scripted message that ran along the inside of his left forearm left her breathless. She hadn't been brave enough to ask what it said. She wanted not to care, not to believe that Brent could have more to him than good looks and fame.

He had bad boy written all over him. The words *danger* and *enter at your own risk* should be worn as a sign across his chest, but the problem was that she'd started to think he was worth the gamble. What was the worst thing that could happen? They'd sleep together and then he'd leave?

Yes, DJ, that's exactly what would happen! He would leave. There was no doubt about it. But there was a small voice in her head that said he'd leave either way, whether she slept with him or not. All Brent had ever offered was a good time. Was she enough of a big girl to accept that?

Sick of the merry-go-round in her head, DJ flung the covers off and padded barefooted into the bathroom. A year after her parents had died Derrek had taken a day off work and surprised her by moving all her stuff into their parents' master suite. When she'd gotten home from school that day she'd been touched and hurt all at the same time. When she confessed as much, he'd simply told her it was time. Their parents weren't coming back, and if he had to continue sharing a bathroom with her, he'd start drinking tequila for breakfast every morning.

DJ smiled at the memory. It was nice to be able to think of her parents without crying. She got dressed, brushed her teeth, applied a liberal amount of sunscreen—freckles being the bane of her existence—and then made her way to the kitchen. She went to pull out the pans for eggs and turkey sausage, but then stopped. She'd forgotten that Derrek had been sleeping on the recliner since after he'd broken his ribs and brought home Emily, a stray nurse from the hospital. Leave it to her brother to find a damsel in distress and take it upon himself to rescue her. Which reminded her—she was supposed to clean out the upstairs guest bedroom, but she kept getting sidetracked and forgetting. Didn't seem that her brother was put out by it none. Seemed he was more than pleased that a pretty little nurse was sleeping in his bed. Too bad it was without him.

She groaned and put the coffee on to brew. Was anyone getting any action around here? No wonder a person could cut the sexual tension in this house with a knife.

"Kitchen duty again? I thought it was my turn," Derrek said, as he shuffled out of the living room, clothes all wrinkled, hair sticking straight up.

"Sorry, I couldn't sleep. I didn't mean to wake you." She let her gaze do a quick glance over him. It was a habit she'd gotten into at a young age, a quick visual check to make sure that he was doing okay.

"You and I both, but I've got a reason. What's your excuse?"

At the mention of his injury, her gaze went to his ribs. He was no longer favoring one side, but that didn't mean anything. Her brother was stubborn about asking for help if nothing else. "How are your ribs?"

He threw her an annoyed look. "The same as they were the last ten times you asked. I'm fine, they're healing, and Emily is doing more than enough worrying for both of you.

At the mention of the pretty, petite nurse who'd come to stay with them because of some unexpected financial issues, DJ wiggled her eyebrows at her brother. She was glad her brother was finally showing interest in someone else. That rich snob Lilly Warrington had done a number on her brother. So glad he hadn't let her ruin him permanently for other women. "Yeah, you don't seem to mind all that nursing she's been giving you. Brent and I have a bet going as to how long you'll be sleeping in that recliner. I see the way you look at her."

Derrek nodded his head, then came around and grabbed his mug from off the hook under the cabinet. "Funny, because Emily and I have a similar bet as to how much longer you're going to be giving Brent the cold shoulder."

DJ quickly opened the fridge to help cut off that particular line of questioning. It was funny when she was teasing him. Not so much the other way around.

Derrek held out his cup for her to pour the creamer in their morning-routine gesture, so familiar that it was similar to a well-choreographed dance "Could it be that this 'thing' between you and Brent is the reason for your sleepless nights?"

She grabbed her own cup, did the half cream, half coffee mix, and then leaned against the counter. Her first instinct was to keep her feelings and thoughts to herself, but this was her brother, and ever since their parents' death, they'd had to learn to rely on each other. "No! This has nothing to do with Brent, but..." She lowered her voice and slipped into stilted speech meant for confessions and secrets. "You were right about something else."

Derrek raised his eyebrows and tried to hide his smile behind his coffee cup. "Do tell. I love it when that happens."

She tried to muster up a smile at his comment, but her lips fell flat as a long expanse of sun-scorched Texas prairie. "I think I need to go and get a life. You're right. Find some friends. Start dating."

Derrek put his cup down. His hand over his heart. "This is serious, DJ," his tone anything but. "You just said the D-word. Wonders never cease."

DJ nodded, the tightening of her throat as surprising as it was unwelcome. What was she being emotional about? She looked at Derrek. He was one of her closest friends, and yet even she wasn't stupid enough to tell him that Brent wanted to sleep with her. She was pretty sure her older brother would have a thing or two to say about her hooking up with the rock star in the bunk house. Brent may be his best friend, but she was his only sister.

Even if it was just a few overused lines, she didn't want anyone to know that she was flattered by Brent's attention. When was the last time someone had called her pretty and asked her for a kiss? Never, that's when, and no one, that's who. "All I'm saying is that maybe I should go out to Everyday Joe's this Friday night. There's no reason I can't go and socialize. I may even pick up a dance or two. I'm not married to these horses, and if I don't do something quick, that's exactly how I'm going to end up—like old Mrs. Pickleninny. You remember her? She used to live on the edge of town and never had any visitors. She only came into town once a month, and then only to buy a liter of Vodka and canned chili."

Derrek shifted in the chair as he tried to find a more comfortable position. His ribs must still be bothering him. "It wasn't because she didn't want any visitors; it was because of all that chili. She bought it by the case."

DJ laughed, but Derrek had a knowing look in his eye that told her he had something up his sleeve.

"Well, you're far from an old lady, and you're allergic to cats, so I don't see that in your future. But I do have a plan to help with this turning of a new leaf." Derrek always had a plan. He was one of those guys that saved for a rainy day, or could be counted on to be the designated driver. When Derrek had a plan, DJ usually had to admit he was right. "I've thought this through, so hear me out before you say no."

"No," she said just out of habit. What was it with all the men in her life telling her to hear them out before she said no? She wasn't that closed-minded.

He just looked at her. "Hey, you want to live with nine

cats and a bowl of chili, that's fine." He grunted as he stood and turned to make his way out.

She rolled her eyes, but tapped her spoon against the rim of the coffee cup to grab his attention. "Fine. I'll listen."

Derrek's lips twitched like the ear of Queenie when she smelled a treat. "Good, because I've already talked this over with Brent."

DJ's good humor evaporated. "You talked what exactly over with Brent?"

His furrowed brow indicated his confusion. "Weren't we talking about the fact that you're lonely and desperate and that you need to start dating?"

DJ's heart dropped, and embarrassment soured her stomach like creamer left in the hot sun. "Oh my God, you told Brent that?"

Derrek smiled, reminding her of the mischievous boy who had relocated the river frogs into their bathtub and hand-fed the family dog his serving of vegetables. "Don't worry, he totally agrees. He understands what happened after mom and dad died, and how that made you a little more..."

Derrek looked at her and gestured for help to come up with the right word.

"Appreciative?" she offered, wishing her brother had been struck mute along with his broken ribs.

"No," he shook his head.

"Kinder."

"Nope, not that either."

"Self-reliant?" Jesus, this was like playing "Name That Tune."

"Oh God, no." He shook his head as if the thought was repugnant to him. "You don't need any more of that. What's the opposite of self-reliant?"

"Needy?" Her voice squeaked up to an octave she hadn't used since she'd been five and realized that My Little Pony was also a cartoon on Saturday mornings. "Oh my God, you told him I was *needy?*"

DJ struggled to keep her voice down, but it was hard. It wasn't like she cared what Brent thought of her. She didn't. He could go to hell. But needy? Anything but needy.

"No." To her relief he shook his head.

"Damn it. I had it... oh..." He snapped, and then did a quick finger-point, as if he'd just perused a thesaurus. "Stubborn."

"Stubborn?" She knew it wasn't a question, but there was so many things wrong with Derrek and Brent's conversation that she was having trouble assimilating all of them.

"Yeah," he nodded. A self-satisfied smile on his face. "Stubborn, closed-off, disengaged."

"Disengaged?" If she continued to repeat everything he said she'd run the risk of him adding stupid to the list, but still. Disengaged. What did that even mean?

Derrek did the traffic-cop stop with his hand in defense. "Listen, don't get yourself all worked up. I'm not criticizing."

"It sounds like you are," she said, her voice pinning each word like a thumb tack to a corkboard. Derrek's face softened like he was working with a feisty horse or trying to calm a scared mare. "I get it, okay. I understand why you're a little self-protective. It's a natural reaction after everything we've been through. I think when we lost mom and dad it was harder for you than me. At least I was an adult, but you, you still needed a woman in the house. There were so many things you were left to find out on your own."

DJ's heat of anger washed away with the last swallow of cold coffee. Talking of what they'd both lost put everything in perspective. "I had you."

And she had. Derrek had been great. She couldn't have asked for a better brother.

Derrek made to go refill his coffee, but DJ shook her head and served him instead. He nodded his thank you, and took his time to blow and sip his coffee before continuing "Listen, I know you and Brent don't see eye to eye on a lot of things. But he's really not such a bad guy."

And like a teeter-totter her anger was back again. She really needed to get some decent sleep. Her emotions were all over the place. "I can't believe you are defending him. The man's been here a little over a couple weeks, and in that time, he got you drunk enough to fall off your horse and break your ribs. He ruined my bedspread and threw up in my truck. He's nothing, but trouble."

He sighed. "Nobody made me drink, Brent sent your bedspread to the dry cleaners, and, well... he said he'd take care of the truck."

She slammed her cup on the counter. "Every time I turn on the AC my truck smells like vomit. Every time I use the AC. We live in freaking hot as hell Texas, Derrek!"

Derrek covered his hands with his face and groaned. "Okay, okay, let's look past that for a moment. What I'm trying to tell you is that he really is an upstanding guy. I know you hold it against him that he never made it to mom and dad's funeral, but he called me in tears as soon as he heard. He was willing to walk off the first real big break he'd gotten to come home and be with me, but I told him no."

DJ inhaled sharp and cutting. "You told him no?"

Derrek nodded, his whole body slumping as if the memory sapped his energy. "Yeah, DJ, I told him if he left the tour he was on I'd kick his ass. You know Brent. Music was, *is*, everything to him. I wasn't going to jeopardize that just so he could hold my hand and get drunk with me after the funeral."

She still didn't believe it. "But he was your best friend. He should've been there."

"And he was. That's what I'm trying to tell you. When mom and dad died, I tried to hide a lot of stuff from you. The bills, the stress of making it on our own, my loneliness. Inside I was devastated. I'd just lost two of the most important people in my life, but you needed me strong. I know you think Brent was a bad influence, but he was the best person for me during that time. He forced me to get out of the house. And for those few weekends Brent flew me out to Nashville to stay with him, I forgot I was solely responsible for another person. Forgot I had to make all the right decisions. I needed those nights. There was a time I needed them so bad that those weekends with Brent were the only thoughts that got me up in the morning. I will always be grateful to him for being there during the hardest time in my life."

DJ turned her back on her brother and braced her palms against the counter. She'd never known all that her brother had gone through. She'd been so caught up in her own grief she'd never thought about how he was dealing. All this time she'd put the blame at Brent's feet for taking her brother away from her, but Brent and Derrek had only been eighteen at the time. Both of them had been kids, really. And while Derrek had taken his responsibilities better than some men twice his age, Brent had done what he could. In retrospect, her judgment against Brent seemed pretty childish.

"I guess what I'm saying is," Derrek's voice sounded careful, as if testing an iced over pond for the first time, "if there's anyone who can help you live life a little, it's Brent. So that's why I asked him to take you out on a date."

DJ groaned and hid her face behind her hands. There was no way she could look Brent in the eye now. Not after her brother set up a pity date for her.

"And just for clarification," Derrek said, as if any type of clarification would help the situation. "I asked him to take you out on a date, not hook up with you. He's my best friend, but I don't like him that much."

DJ whipped around. "Oh, so glad you stopped at prostituting your sister out. That makes me feel a lot better."

Derrek tossed his hands up, sick of her foolishness. "I can see you are just looking for a fight, Danielle. But you know what? It's not going to be with me."

He stood and pushed his stool in under the counter, signaling that the conversation, at least on his end, was over. "You know, Danielle, you're not the only one with heartache from the past. Plenty of people have skeletons in their closets, but they don't use that as an excuse to push people away. They use it as an opportunity to learn. Your choice."

THIRTEEN

*B*rent had been up and was already making breakfast before the crack of dawn. If anyone would've told him that in less than two weeks' time, he'd have changed from his night-owl, partying ways to waking up before dawn, working all day with some smelly horses, then to holing up at home in the evenings to write some of the best songs he'd done in his life, he would've called them crazy. But that's exactly what he was doing. Funny, he should be crying instead of whistling.

Brent smiled, and continued whistling. The physical activity hadn't been so bad. In fact, he'd been in a more creative state of mind lately. With his days filled with physical activity, his nightly writing sessions had become way more productive. With Derrek laid up the last two weeks, there'd been no way Brent could allow DJ to carry all the extra work, especially since he'd been partially responsible.

Brent poured the freshly brewed coffee into a thermos and started the second pot. This ranch ran on hard work and caffeine; no wonder DJ had trouble sleeping. Not that she'd confided in him. Nope, she was barely talking to him, but a guy could hope that at least some of her sleepless nights had something to do with him. His sure had something to do with her.

There'd been no more talk of sex or having a little fun since the afternoon he'd walked back from the hospital, but the tension was in the air. It nearly crackled whenever they were within shouting distance, and he for one was dying. He couldn't remember the last time he'd been this frustrated, but it was more than that. He found himself watching her when he shouldn't, thinking about her when he should be writing, and using her as a muse for all his songs. Well, whatever this thing with DJ was, it seemed to be working. His agent was ecstatic over his latest lyrics. His album was fast coming to a close, and with the studio time already scheduled, his time here was almost over. He'd be leaving soon. He just wasn't sure how he felt about getting back to the big city. All of a sudden the jet-set lifestyle seemed a bit overdone, and his luxury condo in L.A. a tad lonely.

Brent flipped the pancakes and pulled out the bacon and eggs from where he was keeping them warm in the oven. The gang should be down about now, and he wanted all the food on the table, ready to go. He found DJ had even less patience in the morning, and if breakfast wasn't ready she'd been known to pour some coffee in a thermos full of cream and call it good. By his standards she was getting too thin, had dark circles under her eyes, and was going on less than five hours of sleep each night. He wanted to say something. He was worried and concerned, but he'd already overstepped his boundaries in their last conversation, and now they weren't even talking.

He kept waiting for Derrek to say something, but it seemed that he was a little too preoccupied with the newest roommate, and if Brent was any judge, he didn't think Emily would be just a roommate for very much longer.

"Good Lord, if your fans could see you now." Brent looked up to see Derrek striding into the kitchen with too much of a smile on his face for five AM.

Brent didn't lose a beat. He'd learned that with his best friend he couldn't give an inch, or Derrek would tease him no end. He set a plate in front of him. "If they saw me now they'd be even more in love than they already are. Eat this. You need to keep your strength up. You have a whole day of lying around on the couch in front of you."

Derrek groaned and rolled his eyes.

"If I watch any more daytime TV I'm gonna slice my wrists. I'm working outside today even if it kills me. I can at least lead the horses to the work pen, or drive the truck into town to pick up feed."

Brent turned back to the stove and began to put food on another plate for the next person. "And what will your lovely nurse say about that? She seems pretty opinionated when it comes to your health."

Derrek looked up from shoveling food into his mouth. "That's the best part," he said, around a bite of pancake "She had an early shift at the hospital." He smiled. "So I'm good."

Brent laughed, then stepped out of the kitchen to see if DJ was on her way down. If she wasn't up yet he wanted to let her sleep so he could talk to Derrek before she came down. "Hey man, you have a minute?"

"I got all the time in the world, bro. What's up?" Derrek said, not even looking up as he poured extra syrup on his pancakes. Brent had forgotten how the man could put away the food. Good thing Derrek did a lot of physical work, or else he'd be sporting a belly for sure.

Brent made one last check around the corner. "I'm worried about DJ. She seems... stressed."

Derrek shrugged his shoulders. "That's how DJ runs. She's naturally uptight, and Lord help us all, if something doesn't go according to her plan, then she just goes all tight-laced and quiet about it. That's why I wanted you to take her out. Whatever happened with that?"

Brent sighed and sat down in front of his own plate. "That's the problem. Things got a little complicated."

Derrek dropped his fork and gave Brent his full attention. All his light hearted humor was gone. "Complicated how?"

Brent groaned inwardly. He had to step carefully and remember that Derrek was DJ's big brother first and his best friend second. "We had words, that's all, nothing else."

Derrek looked at him, his dark gaze unwavering and serious. "Good, because I'd hate to have to kick my best friend off my ranch because he got confused as to who was a band groupie and who was my family."

Brent wiped his mouth on his napkin, suddenly no longer hungry. God, if he could only see DJ as a band groupie his whole life would be a lot simpler. "See, here's the thing—"

Just then there was a loud rumbling that sounded like a diesel truck was barreling up the circle front drive.

They both looked at the clock. They looked at each other, then jumped up at the same time to investigate. But neither man made it to the front door first. DJ flew down the stairs fully dressed with both her Stetson and work boots on, causing Brent to wonder if she'd had any intention of eating breakfast at all. Was she avoiding him?

"Now, who the hell on God's green earth would think of

making a visit at this hour?" DJ swore a few times as she wrestled with the front deadbolt.

Brent's heart skipped at the sight of her. He had it bad if he thought her grumpiness before her morning coffee was cute. What was wrong with him?

"I swear, if that's Old Man Skinner trying to off load his low-grade rye feed this early in hopes that I'd still be in bed, he's going to have to surgically remove my foot from his a..." her voice trailed off as she stood in the open doorway, staring out across the front porch.

Derrek walked up behind DJ and let out a low whistle. Immediately, Brent knew what had been delivered to the Double D Ranch, and it sure the heck wasn't rye feed.

He hadn't expected his peace offering to arrive this early. When he'd decided to get his gift for DJ, it had been a little bit of an impulse buy, and a little bit because he wanted to fix the got-sick-in-her-truck thing. But also, he'd liked the thought that she'd have something dependable when he was gone. Now that it was here, his gesture seemed a little over the top, and he was surprised at his sudden embarrassment.

Brent walked out and stood next to his best friend and DJ.

There was no mistaking who the Ford F-450 Platinum, 16 inch, dually-wheeled truck with the Double D Ranch custom brand painted on the driver side was for. It was loud, it was ostentatious, it was over the top, and it was...

"Sweet baby Jesus, it's pink!" Derrek spat the last like it was a different type of four letter word.

Brent had never heard such disgust in a man's voice in all his life. Unfortunately, Brent couldn't help but agree. What the world? He remembered specifically stating he wanted the color "ink". Maybe he shouldn't have ordered a custom paint job sight unseen. He definitely did not say pink. Especially this pink. It was...was...

"It's bloody neon." This from Derrek again, who seemed extremely vocal about a gift that wasn't even for him. "I mean, are those freaking sparkles?'

Brent grimaced. It did look a little glittery in the morning light. He knew specifically that he hadn't ordered sparkles. Pink was bad enough, but sparkles? He hadn't even thought trucks came in that color. "I'm sure it only looks like that in a certain light."

Derrek turned toward him. "If by 'in a certain light' you mean the sunlight, oh, well in that case we're good."

The driver got out of the truck with a clipboard, Tank's Autobody Shop printed across his hat. He hitched up his low-hanging jeans and walked up to the porch. He glanced down at the clipboard. "Which one of you is Brent Kane?"

For the first time in his career, Brent didn't want to own up to who he was. He was already calculating how long it would take him to get the truck repainted. Brent finally found the courage to look over at DJ. He'd seen her speechless before, but never like this. Her mouth had dropped into a gaping circle, eyes wide and unblinking.

Brent looked at the autobody guy and then pointed to Derrek. Tentatively, he hustled DJ over to one side so he could speak to her. "DJ, really, we can fix this." He rushed the words, all the while wondering why his heart was pounding. It was just paint. "I..."

She gasped and clasped both hands over her mouth. She murmured something into her palms that he didn't quite catch.

"What?" He leaned closer. "What's that, honey?"

"Is this for me?" Her eyes never left the sparkling pink truck that stood running in the driveway.

"Well, I'm sure the hell not going to be driving it," Derek grumbled behind her.

DJ gasped. Walking off the porch, she slowly made her way down toward the truck. "I don't understand. I don't... why?"

She looked shocked. Brent began to wonder if anyone had ever given her a gift, but he was also a tad bit embarrassed. The gesture was too over the top for mere friends, but maybe he was trying to make up for not coming back that summer when she had needed him the most.

Brent shoved his hands into his pockets. "It's just that the truck you're driving now is a POS, and you're a real rancher, and a real rancher needs a real truck that can haul horse trailers and make you look good doing it."

But he was mostly talking to himself since DJ was already checking out the tailgate and vanity license plate with "#1Rancher" on it.

Out of nowhere, Derek slugged him in the arm—hard. "Not sleeping together, huh? A man only gets a girl a truck if he's getting totally freaky on the side. My sister is a good girl. You better not have gotten her into any of the kinky L.A. stuff, because I swear to God, I'll kill you right here and now."

Brent stepped back and threw his hands in the air. "What? No, Derek, I swear, we're not sleeping together. I promise."

The autobody guy waved his clip board in both of their faces. "Hey, I just need someone to sign for this, and then give me a ride back to the shop, if you could."

Derek shoved Brent hard. "Then what do you want me to believe? Because this truck is a disgrace to God and man. Who the hell paints an F-450... pink? I mean, no guy would do that to a truck unless he's head over heels in love."

Derrek stilled and stared at Brent like he'd just shaved both eyebrows and started spouting poetry. "Oh my God, is that it? Are you in love with Danielle?"

"What? That is so ridiculous. I mean, what are you even saying? You're crazy. I threw up in her car. I'm just replacing it, is all." Brent finally wised up enough to shut up. The more he talked, the worse Derrek's look got. No, he wasn't in love, they barely liked each other, but to explain in words how he felt when he couldn't even figure it out in his head was more than he could handle. He was glad DJ was out of ear shot.

He quickly walked past Derrek and made his way over to DJ. "So...um...what are you thinking right now?"

Hell, did he really just sound like an adolescent boy with his heart in his hands? DJ just stood there, hands over her mouth, eyes wide in a panicked-wild-horse-caught-in-a-pen look. She glanced at him, then turned and made her way around to the side of the truck, out of sight of any onlookers. He followed like a puppy dog that a little girl would bring home from the pet store. He found her standing with her hat pushed low over her eyes, arms crossed, lips pressed into a white line.

"DJ, honey, really, I know this is too much. We can paint it a different color. We can take it back and get you a trac-tor...I don't know, I'm so in over my head, just tell me what you wa..."

She turned, grabbed hold of his shirt, and with the rest of his apology still in his mouth, she kissed him.

The shock almost had him stepping back, but he wasn't a rock star for nothing. He knew how to take an opportunity and run with it. He cradled her face in his palms and angled his mouth so he could kiss her better. Her fingers twisted in his shirt even more, so when she finally broke the kiss her hold never eased.

"Thank you." Her words floated out on a sigh. "I love it. I really *love* it."

Tears shimmered in her dark eyes, making him want to drink from those onyx pools as though she'd cast a spell over him. If she asked him right then and there for his soul, he'd hand it over willingly, even though he knew, *knew*, what she meant when she said the L word. Knew she was talking about the truck, but he couldn't help but wonder what he'd be willing to give up if she said the L word about him.

His gift may've been over the top, but then, so was her reaction. Tears streamed down her cheeks, and there was nothing even close to a smile on her face. In fact, she looked like she was having a real hard time keeping herself together.

"Honey, sweetheart, it's okay. Tell me what's the matter." God, was this even him? He never talked like this, but DJ vulnerable and trembling in his arms made him want to move heaven and earth to make her happy again.

She shook her head, her lips moving on silent words. Finally, she swallowed and found her voice. "I... I mean...why? Why would you do this?"

Now it was his turn to fumble around for words. He wanted to tell her the truth, what was really in his heart, but he also didn't want to hurt her. She hadn't let go of his shirt, and she was really close. He could feel her breasts pushed up against his chest, smell her fresh morning scent, feel the touch of her skin under his palms, and for a moment he slipped under a spell that made him want to make promises he couldn't keep. To build a life there was no way he could live.

But he couldn't do that with DJ. He had to be honest with her, more so than he'd ever been with anyone in his life. His life was full of promises bigger than who he was. He'd built an image of a bigger-than-life rock star, a legend. But he wanted to talk to her as Brent, the man that only she and Derrek knew... not as a rock star, but as an ordinary man would talk to a woman. "I want to tell you the truth, but I can't if you keep looking at me like that."

She stared up at him with more emotions in her eyes than he'd ever felt in a lifetime. He didn't deserve her, not a woman like DJ. "Like what?"

He wouldn't hurt her this time, as he had back when he hadn't understood that kisses were like promises unsaid. He made that mistake once when she was young and he'd been stupid. He didn't want to do that again. "Like you see a better man than I am."

"And what kinda man is that?" The words tumbled from her lips like leaves in a wind storm. Then she answered her own question. "One that is as stable and sure as the rising sun? One I know will be here for me? One whose promises are like a steadfast oak, whose heart is complete?"

He nodded, surprised at the tightness in his throat, the weight of emotion heavy on his chest. Why the hell did he want to be that man? Why did he think that with her in his arms—her breath on his cheek, her lips a mere whisper away from his—that he had a chance of being that man? "Yeah, that look."

Her lips trembled into an upturned smile for the first time since she'd awakened and flung open the door this morning. She pulled him down to meet her half way, and just before she kissed him, she whispered against his mouth the sweetest words he'd ever heard. "Nah, I'm more of the rock star, playboy type myself."

FOUTEEN

*D*J drove her new F-450 on her way home from the mall, loving the way the truck handled and the power of the V8 engine she knew would make towing a trailer a breeze. Today for the first time she could remember, she'd cut out of work early and headed into town for some much-needed shopping and pampering.

She glanced at the pink and white striped bag sitting on the seat next to her, and worried her bottom lip. *What was she doing? Was she really this much of an idiot?*

She glanced in the rearview mirror to avoid answering, instead checked out her new hairdo for the umpteenth time. She'd forgotten how good it felt to get her hair cut and blown-out. She promised, from now on she'd make more time for herself, that was one thing if nothing else that having Brent back home had reminded her of.

Brent ... the thought of him made her heart race and palms sweat like she was some kind of hormone-induced teenager. She sure felt like one.

The sun set hours ago, but the night was still early which was why she was surprised to see flashing red and blue lights from the squad car outside Everyday Joe's. She slowed down to take in the scene, then recognizing the jet-black truck and custom wheels, she groaned and turned into the parking lot.

"That's some truck," Deputy Allan VanBrandt's said, when she walked up and gave him a greeting.

"I know, isn't she a beauty?" DJ couldn't help but gush. She'd been soaring high on all the stares and gasps she'd been getting in town. But from the look on the deputy's face, she wasn't sure if he would agree with her, so she rushed into why she stopped in the first place. "So..." she gestured toward the patrol car. "Is he in there?"

"Yep..." Allan said, not having to confirm who "he" was. "Had to place him under arrest this time. Joe finally got fed up."

DJ nodded, not at all surprised. Joe was usually a laid-back dude, so it had to have been bad if he'd called the cops. "What happened this time?"

Allan shrugged. "Same as what happens all the time. He got drunk, started berating the waitresses, and Joe asked him to leave."

"And let me guess...he didn't go nicely."

There was a half-grunt, half-snort from the deputy. "Does *he* ever do anything nicely?"

DJ sighed, that question didn't need answering. "What's going to happen to him?"

"I'm going to take him the station, hold him there over night until he sobers up, and then charge him a hefty fine. Hey...wanna ride with me?" Allan asked, real hope in his voice.

Dread washed over DJ. She knew why Deputy VanBrandt had asked her to come along. Chandler Sloan was a notorious asshole, but for whatever reason when she was around, he simmered down. Not nice exactly, no, but less of a dick...sorta.

DJ glanced back toward her new truck, the thought of her recent purchase on the passenger side, her new haircut, her freshly painted nails. She had other plans for tonight, ones that didn't include angry drunk men. "No thank you, but..." she continued when Allan's face dropped. "Let me talk to him."

Deputy VanBrandt nodded with more enthusiasm than she felt, and walked her over to the police car, letting her in the backseat.

DJ closed the door behind her, and then stared at the broken man sitting next to her.

He was big, six-foot something, wide shoulders, broad arms that took up more than his fair share of the backseat. Fine with DJ, she had no plans of staying here long. "Chandler," she said, when he didn't look up at her.

His head was bowed, dark hair falling over his face, all the indications of a guilty conscience, but she knew better... it was because of his wrists handcuffed behind his back.

"Chandler." She had to at least get him to look at her or this was going to take a hell of a lot longer than she was willing to spend. "Berating a poor waitress... a new low even for you."

Blood-shot, grey-blue eyes peered out from underneath strands of ropey black hair. His five-o'clock shadow already making a play for a full-out beard. "You weren't privy to the service. She should be fired."

"Please." She rolled her eyes. "You should know better." Everyday Joes wasn't known for its stellar service since Joe, the owner, hired staff more on who he wanted to sleep with than on any skill on the waitresses' part. "She'll probably quit, thanks to you."

"Works for me also," his tone sharp and not at all slurred from drink.

So, he wasn't drunk. He was pissed. Not an unusually occurrence, but one that took a different approach to deal with than drunk Chandler.

"What happened?" She asked not because she actually cared—she didn't. And not because she didn't already know —she did. But because Chandler needed someone to gripe to and for some reason, only God knew why, she was that person.

And gripe he did. About the waitress, about Joe, about his brother, about his mother, about his father, but never, *ever* about the one person who he really hated. Nope, never about the person whose-name-shall-not-be-uttered.

DJ admired her freshly done nails, a real luxury for her. She'd kept them short, but had wanted the color to match her new truck. Pretty darn close, maybe not as much sparkle, but close.

She rolled her gaze toward Chandler. Still talking. She patted her hair and wondered how long she could go before she had to wash the style out.

After a few minutes, she tuned an ear toward Chandler. He was saying something about his father. Good, which meant he was close to being done. His father always came last in his long list of people who'd done him wrong.

DJ went back to daydreaming about Brent, and what he'd say when he saw her. Unlike some men—she spared a glance toward Chandler—Brent would always notice when she got her hair and nails freshly done.

"And over and over he begs me to make her come back, to make her come back home."

That snapped DJ back to the present. She was pretty sure she knew who the "her" was in that sentence, but his father must have gotten bad in order to have begged his first-born son for anything. "I take it he's not doing well."

Chandler shook his head. "The doctor gave him three months, maybe six at best."

DJ reached out and clasped his arm. "I'm sorry."

Chandler ignored her touch. They both knew hers wasn't the touch he longed for.

DJ took a deep breath like one would before diving into a cold ocean...and jumped in. "And did you...call her? Is she coming?"

The silence all the more profound after Chandler's talking. Even in the dim lighting, DJ could see the flex of Chandler's jaw—sharp enough to cut, hard enough to kill.

The violence crackled, filling the small cab, and DJ withdrew her hand.

Finally, as if grabbling with self-control he so rarely showed these days, Chandler shook his head. "After all I've done for her, after all that we *were*, she doesn't even have the decency to return my phone calls."

And DJ understood, because underneath all the anger and the hate was a heartbreak so deep and wide, she feared Chandler would never be whole again.

FIFTEEN

*I*f DJ had checked herself in the mirror once, she'd done it a hundred times. *Holy Crap.* The image that stared back at her was frightening, daring, and totally out of her realm. She quickly closed the long rancher's trench coat over her body, then groaned out loud. She was a walking cliché—long coat, high heels, and sexy lingerie underneath, but there was a reason why it was cliché... it worked. The plan was to get from her house to the bunk house without anyone seeing her, and the long coat masked her true intentions. Well, if one didn't notice the three-inch stilettos while she tramped though the mud.

When she'd left Chandler in the backseat of the squad car, she had all but nixed her late-night plan of seduction. But by the time she'd gotten home, she'd changed her mind back again. Maybe it had been the look on Chandler's face, or the pity on Deputy Allan VanBrandt's or just the fear that if she didn't change something there was a very real possibility she'd end up just like the bitter, angry, and alone, Chandler Sloan.

DJ let her head fall into her hands. This was ridiculous. Why was she standing here in her bathroom late at night contemplating a rash, superficial, laughable, and totally insane fling with the womanizing rock star that was holed up in her bunkhouse a few yards away?

Three words: stupid, pink, and truck.

Who would've thought she'd been that easy. For all her tough talk and swagger about playboys and independence, one grand gesture and she was a goner. Just like that. The truth was if it had been anything else—jewelry, flowers, or a trip to Paris–she would've thumbed her nose in his direction and laughed. *Okay, maybe not the trip to Paris.* But a truck. That truck was exactly, kinda, really what she needed to run this ranch, and for some reason him knowing what she needed had touched her heart on some deep level. *Did* he really know her?

DJ's spine straightened in denial. No, don't go there. This... this... thing with Brent was not about that. Brent had, in no uncertain terms, told her he was not long term. He'd told her he was fun only. No strings attached. Like her momma always said, when people tell you who they are, believe them. So if she was going to go through with this she needed to go with her eyes wide open.

But why even risk having her heart broken again?

DJ leaned against the bathroom counter and let the coat hang down her back. It was only, like, ninety degrees, and even with the AC, her overcoat had started to make her sweat.

Why? Because she wasn't getting any younger, that's why, because she needed a bit of fun in her life, and because this... this may be her last chance to do something spontaneous. Every year she kept her head down and nose to the grindstone made it harder and harder to remember the girl who used to play, have fun, and believe in happy endings.

There wasn't a day that went by that she didn't think of how her life would've changed if her parents hadn't died that night. If she closed her eyes she could see her parents, as real to her as her four-legged porcelain bathtub, or the print copy of the Monet her mother had gotten on her honeymoon trip to France that was hanging over the tub. She pictured her parents the way she remembered them best—out on their boat.

Her parents had gone fishing like most people in Somewhere went to church. Their Bible had been the wide, open expanse of blue Texas sky; their hymn the soft lap of water against the sides of the boat. They had dragged her along when she'd been too young to stay at home alone. But it hadn't taken that many years before she'd started to beg her parents to leave her behind with Derrek. As a child she'd thought there was nothing as boring as a full day of drifting aimlessly around in a boat, but now, as an adult, she wished she hadn't been so hasty to reject their invitation.

"You couldn't have helped them. The accident would've taken you, too," Derrek had said, when she told him she wished she'd been there.

There wasn't much of a chance when a row boat went head on with a high-performance speed boat. No one was exactly sure what had happened, but during the autopsy the other boater had been found to have a high blood-alcohol content.

That was one of the many reasons she'd always had such a problem with Brent. Ever since she'd known him, he'd been a risk taker, a dare-devil, never playing it safe, totally opposite of everything she wanted in her life. He would call up Derrek out of the blue, like an unpredictable summer storm, and Derrek would go barreling over to the wild side like he didn't have a sister at home depending on him.

She knew better than anyone how a simple Sunday spent fishing could end up in tragedy, and yet, look at her now. She was dressed in some new lingerie that she'd specifically gone into town to get just so she could seduce Brent. She wanted to prove to herself, and to him, that she could be bold and daring, a little wild, and that everything would still turn out okay. But what if it didn't?

What was she doing? This was *so* not like her. Once she made a decision she barely ever second-guessed herself. She'd committed herself to this. Heck, look how she was dressed for Pete's sake, she damn well better be committed. This was a time for action, not for hiding in bathrooms. DJ turned on her heel, wrapped her coat around herself, and made her way to the kitchen. So what if she needed to stop and pour herself a shot of tequila to settle her nerves? No one else had to know.

She didn't turn on the porch light as she went through the back door. It was better if no one saw her. The last thing she needed was to explain why she looked like a flasher to her brother and Emily. The stars were out in full force, enriching the sky to a color of deep blue instead of mere black, while a mild summer breeze pushed and pulled the scents of her beloved ranch around her—hay, Texas soil, and horse. She wobbled precariously across the soft earth, the heels of her shoes sinking like tent stakes into the mud.

She made it to the bunkhouse without falling, glad no one was around to witness her graceless trek. The bunkhouse window was slightly ajar, lamp light and the soft strums of guitar music streaming through the opening. Brent was still up. She raised her hand to knock, then thought better of it. No one had seen her. Brent hadn't heard her. She could still turn back without anyone being the wiser. She lowered her arm to her side. All of a sudden thoughts of a cold shower and reruns of CSI Miami seemed a much better plan.

And a much safer one at that.

SIXTEEN

*B*rent laid on his bed, guitar flung across his lap, staring at the ceiling. If people knew how uninspiring it was to watch a song artist write songs, nobody would want to be a rock star. The one line in this lyric was bloody killing him, but instead of trying to figure out what rhymed with "time" he was thinking of how damn hot it was in this crappy bunkhouse.

Maybe he should've saved the money he'd spent on DJ's truck, and put a real AC in this room instead of the pathetic window unit that whirled like a small airplane engine. Then he remembered the look on DJ's face, and how her dark eyes heated like fiery onyx, and her mouth got all pouty and soft, and how she'd kissed him, her fingers gripping his shirt, chest to chest, hip to hip and he knew that no amount of AC would keep him cool.

Freaking DJ. Damn, he couldn't remember the last time he'd had the hots for someone this bad. Just the thought of her got his heart pumping and so turned on that he was literally sick with the need.

He'd almost had her, too. It hadn't been long before

they'd both been panting by the side of the truck, her back flush against the passenger door, his hand lifting her knee up to his hip. He broke the kiss and was one breath away from flinging her over his shoulder and taking her back to the bunkhouse. She must've read the intention on his face because she immediately shook her head and hit his arm to release her. "No, no, Derrek is here. I can't do what's racing though that dirty mind of yours."

All he'd thought was *screw Derrek*. He could go to hell for all Brent had cared, but DJ had taken advantage of Brent's distraction and disengaged herself. She pulled away, straightened her shirt and hair, and basically tried her best not to look like she'd just gotten good and thoroughly kissed.

Brent smiled at the memory. *Not a chance, sweetheart. By the time I'm done with you, you'll be ruined for any other man.*

The thought had him groaning for the umpteenth time. Of course, he was lying here alone, DJ nowhere to be found. She'd quickly left, mumbling excuses about ranch hands, horses, and supplies to order. He'd seen her for about five minutes at dinner, where she'd wolfed down her food standing up and then had taken off, saying she had to run an errand in town.

He'd been a little disappointed when she didn't invite him to come along, but he'd bide his time. A woman didn't kiss a man like that without a hard need burning in her gut for the rest of the day. Lord knows, it was time someone else walked around here in a constant state of arousal.

He had taken off his shirt since it was so damn hot, but now even his jeans were feeling uncomfortable. He closed his eyes and set his guitar down by his bed. This was getting ridiculous. He needed to make a move or he was going to lose his mind. Just then a knock sounded on his door. His heart did a hop and then hard lurch. He took five seconds to send a prayer heavenward. *Dear God, if this has to be Derrek on the other side of my door in the middle of the night, please let it be because he's escorting his sister to my room.*

He sat up straighter and called out, "Enter."

And then there she was, standing just inside his room in the ugliest cattleman's coat ever, and the world's sexiest heels, and it took everything he had to keep his cool and not jump up and do a fist pump in the air. But no matter how cool he acted, he couldn't help the huge grin that broke across his face. "Hi."

Holy hell, was he breathless already? Didn't matter, her smile matched his, and he was just about ready to float off this bed.

"Hi," she said, with one hand braced on the door jam and the other fiddling with the middle button of her coat. "So, have you ever been a booty call from a bona fide rancher?"

His breath left him in a rush. "I swear to God, only in my dreams, but I'm all for making that fantasy a reality."

She flipped her long, dark hair off her shoulder in some kind of sexy head swivel, and placed her hand on an out thrust hip. "Well now, here's your chance. Because, you know, ranchers do it better than anyone else, even rock stars."

"Better than rock stars? Really?" He loved this conversation, he loved this bunkhouse, loved the crappy air conditioner that was going to make it impossible for her to keep that coat on, and he loved every word coming from her pouty, juicy mouth.

"Oh yeah," she said, with a wave of her hand. "Ranchers get it on all the time. At the pastures, at the feed store, down at the stables, all over the place. You know, we ranchers get around."

At the feed store?" He shook his head confused. "Really?"

She winced. "Okay, wait. That didn't come out exactly how I wanted."

He ran his hands through his hair, dying to jump off this bed and attack her. "This is crazy. Why are we still talking?"

"Wait, hold on." She held up a finger, stepped back outside, and closed the door.

Without a second to lose, Brent dove off the bed and into his dresser. He grabbed his old shirt to swipe under his arms, did some quick deodorant action, and then jumped back into bed into what he hoped was his super cool, nonchalant pose.

DJ walked back in, and this time made it all the way to where she could lean back against the opposite wall. She swallowed, and he could tell she was nervous. He'd never seen anything more endearing. "Hi."

"Hi," he said, his smile way wider this time around. Crap, he wrote words for a living. One would think that he could come up with something more profound than "hi." He wanted to sweet talk her, get up and pull her over to him, lay her down on the bed and make sure there wasn't another rational thought in her brain for the rest of the night. But he also wanted this to be her decision. He needed her to acknowledge that she wanted this.

They both stared at each other. She broke first. "I'm just gonna skip my whole line about ranchers and rock stars. It wasn't that funny to begin with. I'll cut to the chase."

His eyes feasted on her. Even in the big overcoat, he could see a great pair of legs peeking out. "I'm all about cutting to the chase. Everything pre-chase is awful. Terrible. No one should ever mess around with 'before the chase.'"

She nodded, her smile lost to the wicked abuse her teeth gave her lower lip as she took a few steps toward him and then hesitated. He saw exactly when she lost her nerve. She glanced down, then back up, and a blush flushed her face. "Um... are you... I mean, this could've been a mistake..."

She'd come far enough. There was no way he was going to let her go. He was up and half way across his room before she could even blink. He grabbed her around the waist and pulled her down onto the bed next to him. "If this is a mistake, then this is one you're gonna make."

She smiled up at him, her cheeks still red, but her eyes danced beneath the long lashes. He knew she was waiting for him to make the next move—bend down, kiss her, say something smooth and charming, but he didn't. For a long moment, all he wanted to do was stare at her; look down at her with his arm holding her tight to his side as he finally accepted that his fantasies were coming true. He wanted to take this moment and savor it, because he was happy. So happy. He couldn't remember a time when he'd been this satisfied with his life. There was just him, DJ, and his music, and a quiet voice told him this was all he'd ever need.

He pushed a dark strand of hair from her face, and then let his gaze travel down her body—or, at least, what he could see of her.

"This is the ugliest coat I have ever seen." He couldn't keep the sincerity out of his voice. If she'd told him she'd gotten it out of the Salvation Army's lost and found pile, he wouldn't have doubted it.

Her eyes widened in shock. "What? This coat? It's my favorite. I've had it since junior high."

He nodded. "It looks it. But please tell me that you have

something under this god awful thing that's as sexy as those high heel shoes you're wearing."

She smiled at him like she knew a secret that only he had a chance of ever finding out. "Maybe. I guess you'll have to take a look and see."

That was the best invitation he'd ever heard. He didn't have to be told twice. He quickly reached over and unbuttoned the coat. Underneath she wore a black lace bra with pink trim, and the sexiest black lace undies he'd ever seen, with a tiny pink bow attached to the front. His mouth watered. "Wow," he sighed, leaning over her so he could take in the scents of honeysuckle and fresh cut grass from his long unfilled fantasies of an adolescent boy that mingled with those of the full grown man. "You are the most beautiful woman I have ever seen."

She looked up at him through dark tinted lashes. Lips in a slightly open pout. Skin brown sugar soft. "Wow, doesn't it bother your conscience to lie that easily?"

"I'd never lie to you, Sugar."

"Somehow, I find that I believe you."

"Believe this," he said, just before he took her mouth and captured her breath with his lips. The taste of her was the same as when he'd had her by the stables and the side of the truck. It was as enticing now as it was then. A mix of vanilla and tequila, of sweetness and provocativeness. He wondered how he'd ever get enough, and they'd only just begun.

His tongue danced with hers in a rhythmic prelude of what was to come. The kiss went from fun and flirty to deep and wanting with startling speed. He broke away to find the soft skin just below her neck. He needed a way to slow things down, or this moment would be over before it even began. DJ arched her back as each of her breaths come quicker and quicker.

"I love this bra," he said, as he licked and nipped between the lace and the underside of her breasts. "In fact, it's the king, or is it the queen, of all bras. In the land of bras, it's the goddess that needs to be worshiped, but I would like nothing more right now than to take this off and throw it across the room. Are you okay with that?"

She nodded, frustration coming through in the small low moans in the back of her throat. "Why are you still talking?"

He took the hint, shut his mouth, and unclasped her bra with one hand—a skill learned in high school, and one that had come in handy ever since. Ample and full, he had no idea these were what waited for him underneath all those tight tank tops. If he'd known, he would've instituted a wet tee-shirt contest the day she made him muck out all the stalls.

His mouth feasted and it wasn't long before her moans became quick, her breathing hard, and her back began arching off the bed. And he was just getting started. He traveled down to her stomach and tasted the moist, brown sugar skin that he couldn't seem to get enough of.

DJ was fit, there was no doubt about it. She spent hours each day doing physical labor on the ranch, most of the time forgoing any meal besides coffee in a large silver mug. Her stomach was concave and muscled from years of horseback riding and hard work. The result was a body that made his mouth water and fantasies explode.

He was used to supermodels with their rail-thin forms, and groupies with their plastic surgery and bleached blonde hair. Nothing in his life had prepared him for DJ. She was real, strong, and completely genuine. Just the feel of her skin beneath his lips was enough to blow his mind.

"Aren't you a little overdressed for this event?" Her voice

a contradiction of casualness and breathy need, and he loved the fact that he was doing that to her.

He couldn't agree more. They both were. Then she was lying there. DJ, the girl who had had a crush on him, the woman that had never wanted him, was now in his bed with nothing but a blush framed by an ugly brown coat—an image he would remember until he was a hundred years old.

She was beautiful.

Brent wrote poetry for a living. At least, that's how he liked to think of his music. But for the life of him, he couldn't think of one line, one word, that would describe what he was feeling at this moment.

So he let his actions speak. He began to make love *to* her. And Brent didn't do that with women. He didn't have to. Most of the time—okay, all of the time—he was the recipient not the giver. Sure, he was considerate— he wasn't that big of a jerk—but it wasn't like he went out of his way, or even wanted to go out of his way, to make sure his partner was happy.

But with DJ it was different. *He* was different when he was with her. He wanted to please her. He wanted to make *her* happy.

"Brent. Brent." His name tumbled from her lips like others uttered prayers, and he felt himself falling with every syllable she uttered. "Kiss me."

With pleasure. And he did. He took his time. Slow in the beginning. He wanted their first time to be good—something she'd never forget. Neither of them would.

"Brent?"

Was she speaking? He didn't even think he could form a coherent thought, much less answer her. And God help him if she was going to tell him she wanted to change her mind.

He was prepared to use all his sweet talking charm in order to convince her to stay right here where she belonged.

"Brent?" she said again, demanding his attention.

He grunted.

"When we're done.... can we do this again?"

He smiled and sighed a breath of relief. God, he loved her. "Oh yeah. Don't you know rock stars can go all night?"

Her smile shone in her eyes, and like sunlight bouncing off a still pond, she blinded him. "Good, 'cause so can ranchers."

SEVENTEEN

*T*he sun had long ago filtered in through the windows, informing her that daylight was a-wasting, and yet they still hadn't gotten out of his bed. Even with the sheet having long ago found its way to the floor, her skin moistened with sweat, and sporting a bad case of bed-head, she couldn't have cared less while lying side by side with Brent, completely spent and satisfied.

Sounds of the ranch in full swing floated through the partially cracked window: trucks pulling in and out, horses neighing, and her ranch hands calling out and joking with each other. She groaned and threw her arm across her eyes. "Derrek is going to be so pissed."

Brent laughed, completely comfortable as naked as the day he'd been born. He was spread out on top of the covers, hands behind his head, a full, gloating smile on his face. The man had no shame. Of course, sporting the body that he did, maybe it was more of a shame to cover him up. "Do you really think he's going to kick my butt for sleeping with his little sister? He may just thank me for getting you out of your grumpy mood."

She smacked him with the back of her hand. His stomach contracted with a loud *umph*. "No, he's going to be more pissed off that I missed work. I really need to go. I *really* need a shower."

Brent rolled over onto his side, propping his head up on one hand, and stared down at her. She let her gaze linger with his. Lord, he was beautiful. His shaggy blonde hair caressed his face. The blue of his eyes seemed brighter under the veil of long lashes, and his right bicep flexed under his weight, showing off the intricately designed tattoo that snaked around his arm. She traced the pattern with her finger. Woven artistically on his forearm were the words from his first number one hit song.

> *Place me like a seal over your heart, like a seal on*
> *your arm;*
> *For love is as strong as death,*
> *Its jealousy unyielding as the grave.*
> *It burns like blazing fire, like a mighty flame.*

"I remember when this song came out. I always thought the words were the most beautiful I'd ever heard," she said, letting her fingers feel the lyrics as if they were done in Brail and not ink.

A bashful smile played at his lips. "I didn't write that, you know. I stole it from the most poetic book in the bible, The Song of Solomon."

"It speaks of a romantic heart. I would've never pegged you for having one." Now it was her turn to be bashful. This was not a conversation to have after a fun romp in the sheets.

He traced a line from the top of her collarbone to the bottom of her navel. "You don't know everything about me. There's no way I could write love songs without falling in love." He placed a light kiss on her bellybutton. "Didn't I tell you all rock stars are romantics at heart?"

She didn't like this conversation. She couldn't lie next to a gorgeous man in bed after an incredible night and talk about love and romance. She may be a realist, but her heart wasn't made of stone. She grabbed the sheet off the floor, breaking the mood. "And didn't I tell you all ranchers are pragmatic? I need to get to work."

If he was hurt by her abrupt change in mood, she couldn't tell. Instead, he eyed her wrapped in the sheet like he couldn't wait to remove it. "When was the last time you took a day off?"

"Never."

"I think you deserve one."

She rolled her eyes before letting her mouth warm into a smile. "See, I was right, you are a bad influence."

"But you love me anyway," he said, grabbing her hand and bestowing a small kiss to her open palm.

She wasn't sure if it was the intimate gesture or his words, but the protective shield around her heart cracked open. She knew Brent, knew he threw around words like *love* with little or no thought. He was so open with his feelings, so reckless. She couldn't be that careless. She wasn't like him, as fickle as the sun on a cloudy day. She couldn't let his words make a dent in her heart when she knew his feelings could change just as easily. She'd known the score before she came last night and needed to remember this was nothing but a good time.

"What are you thinking about right now?" he asked, his

blue eyes warming her skin more effectively than any sunbeam could.

"I was just thinking about how I can understand why your fans love you." He asked and she lied. A great basis for a long term relationship, *not*.

"Really? And why is that?" He asked as if he really wanted to know. Could it be that he wasn't as confident as he seemed?

"Because you really are cute. I mean, I can understand why women just want to look at you. No matter what comes out of your mouth, I could just stare all day." She couldn't believe she'd said that, but his openness was rubbing off on her.

"Well, ditto to you," he said, as he brushed his lips against the underside of her wrist.

She rolled her eyes. "Oh no, you can't take my line, turn it around and use it on me. You have to come up with your own."

He laughed and rolled over onto his back, releasing her. "Ugh, I don't think I can come up with anything. Besides, I've already gotten you, no need to sweet talk you any longer."

She gasped and smacked him hard on his stomach.

He grunted. "Hey."

"You deserved it. For a songwriter, you sure don't have a way with words," she teased. She had no idea that things could be so easy between them. She had no idea it could be this fun, this happy. She shut those thoughts down. She couldn't afford to think of herself as happy.

"I think you've pegged me wrong," he sighed contentedly. "I'm more of a man of action than words. Didn't I prove that last night?"

She stared up at the ceiling. More than anything, Brent

needed a dose of humility. "That was last night. What have you done for me lately?"

They both laughed. "Oh my God, I've created a diva. From rancher to diva in the span of one night. A record even for me, but I've got to keep my woman happy, so I have a plan. How about you stay here and hide out from Derrek, and I'll go to the house and bring us some coffee. Or bring myself some coffee and you some hot cream with a dash of coffee?"

She watched him roll out of bed and pull on his jeans, commando style. "And what am I supposed to do while you get breakfast?"

He pulled the sheet up higher around her neck and tucked it in. "Get some rest, because I'm not done with you yet."

He kissed her on the forehead, grabbed his boots, and was out the door.

DJ lay there and stared out after him. A man who looked just as good the 'morning after' as he did the night before, and knew exactly how she liked her coffee... She gnawed at her lip. Who knew sleeping with a rock star would be so detrimental to her heart?

Brent finished buttoning his shirt as he made his way over to the house, the morning sky a come-hither blue that shone for young lovers after the sweet taste of pleasurable nights. The warm heat of the sun on his face along with the knowledge of a good woman in his bed, he knew, was the reason for the stupid grin on his face.

A few of the ranch hands called out a greeting, and Brent waved back. It was crazy how quickly he'd found himself falling into the rhythm of this place. For a man who rarely stayed in one town for more than a night, he was surprised the wanderlust wasn't taking hold.

In the kitchen, he found his way around with ease, not at all minding the simple task of making coffee and scrambling up some eggs and toast for himself and DJ. Back at his loft, he rarely ever cooked. On the road he ate out, but in L.A. there didn't seem to be a need to make a full meal just for himself.

He glanced around the small but comfortable kitchen and realized he felt more at home here than even in his own place in L.A., and for some reason that shocked him more than even DJ showing up in his room last night.

What the hell was he thinking? Was he really seeing himself here, on some two-bit ranch in the very town he'd almost killed himself to get away from?

The thought made his fingers tremble and the skin go taut along the back of his skull. No, he'd worked and sacrificed too much to get the career he had now. There was no way he wanted to go backwards. Did he? He put the eggs back in the carton before he'd even cracked them against the side of the pan. He had no business cooking breakfast for DJ like he was her boyfriend, or like what they had done meant more than he'd expected it to.

His album was almost finished, and he was scheduled to be in the recording studio in a few weeks with a world tour scheduled for later this year. He had no business playing house with someone he cared about as much as he did DJ.

He hadn't expected this hiatus from his life to resonate with something so deep inside him. This vacation wasn't supposed to change him. It wasn't supposed to make him look at his life and figure out what was missing.

A sickening feeling grew in his gut, and the thought of

eating made him sick. He turned off the stove and braced himself against the counter top. He didn't want this. He didn't want to be domesticated. If he wasn't careful, the next thing he knew he'd end up in some kind of long term relationship with a woman that he lov...

He shook his head and stopped his thoughts right there. No, that wasn't what he wanted. Of course, he refused to take in the fact that just moments ago he was deliriously happy, angling his face toward the sun like some kind of besotted fool.

He knew that if he stayed any longer he wouldn't want to leave. And that was a big problem. Because he needed to leave. He needed to get back to his life. He'd made the decision years ago to be married to his work, and there was simply no room for anything else.

He needed to get out now, before he found that there was nothing he wanted to go back to.

EIGHTEEN

*hree months later*

The rain came down in sheets, darkening the sky and dropping the temperature to a chilly sixty-two degrees. DJ slowed down her brand new truck and turned on her high beams. Traversing the farm to market road was slow going in good weather, but in these conditions it was almost faster to walk.

She shouldn't even be out in this weather. She should be at home tucked under her covers with her CSI re-runs, but just last week she'd made Derrek a promise that she'd try harder to get out and meet people, thus the trip to the next town over where the Jane Austin Book Club was being hosted.

In retrospect, she should've ditched the whole thing.

Look what happened the last time you tried to live life to the fullest.

She ground her teeth at the futility of her thoughts as

they always went back to the same thing. Or same person. It had been three months since the night Brent and she had made love, and he had left to make her breakfast in bed.

That afternoon she'd awakened to an empty room with a cold cup of coffee on the bedside table and a quickly scrawled note that read...

So sorry something came up. Breakfast is on me next time.
BK
Yeah, right. Like there'd ever be a next time.

DJ shook her head, disgusted with herself. Anger had been her first reaction, and under the circumstances, a very normal one, but that wasn't how she wanted to spend her life.

No, it was past time that she was honest with herself. She'd known who Brent was, went into the relationship with him with her eyes wide open. He'd never lied to her, never told her he was a guy who'd stick around, or that he'd make her happy. He told her he was the fun-time guy. She'd been the one who'd let the hope of her foolish fifteen-year-old heart spring to life and take root. For some reason, she had still clung to the belief that she was special and that things with her would be different.

Lesson learned.

So yeah, the first few weeks she'd been angry, and then after that the sadness came. She preferred the anger. Derrek was kind enough not to mention anything. If he'd thought that his best friend leaving in the middle of the day without a goodbye was odd, he didn't say anything.

But Derrek wasn't stupid. He knew something had happened.

DJ was just so ready to move on and be over him. Get over the hurt and get on with finding the one she was supposed to spend the rest of her life with. Hence, the miserable trek to a lonely woman's book club.

The radio station went to commercial. Over the last few months she'd taken to listening to talk radio. The thought of hearing one of Brent's songs about true love or good times had been enough to push her over the edge. She flipped through the preset stations, ready for a little music, not at all up to hearing someone yak at her about one more product or service she didn't need.

The radio disk-jockey's voice pierced through the dark cab, the cheerfulness in direct opposition to the somberness of DJ's mood.

"And now, ladies and gentleman, the moment I've been promising all day long. Here's the first cut from Brent Kane's new album *All About You*. I have to say, this one seems a throwback to some of his early stuff, very soulful and sweet. Very unlike the more pop influence of his last album. Tell me what you think. Here's the latest song from Brent Kane, *Love Walked In*."

Chords of music drifted through the truck's cab. The acoustics of the state-of-the-art sound system wrapped her in a spell against her will.

Love walked in with a pair of sexy shoes and an ugly coat
I got scared
Afraid of what my life would be; you being with me

Pain shot through DJ's heart. In the small cocoon of the cab, Brent's familiar rich voice seeped into her skin, vibrated her cells to a whole new frequency. The emotion was so overwhelming, with shaking hands, she pulled over to the side of the road and put the truck into park.

Love walked in with rumpled hair and a sexy smile
With sparkly eyes and quick one-liners
I got scared, afraid you wouldn't see the man you thought
me to be

Rain coursed down the windows in small jagged streams. With the heater full blast and the windshield fogging, she got lost in the moment of his being here, singing just to her as if they were the only two people in the whole world.

I still remember the first time we kissed. I was eighteen
and you were far younger
I felt it then and I know it now,
You are my future, let me show you how

The tears came then. She didn't even try to stop them. Her fingers gripped the steering wheel like a life line out of hell, and yet she wouldn't trade this moment, this song, for anything else in the world.

Now, I got to tell you baby...
Love's walking in with a pair of ugly boots and this here,
worn guitar
But I'm not scared any longer
Please forgive me, I won't leave again
Because of you I've never felt stronger

The song went on. The chorus repeated, but DJ, wasn't able to ignore her pain any longer, rested her head on the steering wheel and sobbed.

It took DJ almost a half hour to pull herself together. By the time she stopped crying and felt sane enough to drive, the rain had let up to a light drizzle and the night reached full dark.

Forty-five minutes later, she pulled up into her driveway. From the comfortable vantage point inside her truck, she could see the porch light had been left on, and a dark form sat in the rocker by the front door.

Even before she turned off the car and made her way across the muddied yard, she knew who was sitting there waiting for her. The only part she hadn't expected was how her heart leapt at the sight.

DJ slowly made her way up the front steps, no longer caring that the light drizzle had dampened her hair and shirt. She needed the time to sort out her feelings. The internal war battled within her; her heart wanted her to run flying into his arms as her brain urged caution, saying their separation was for the best.

By God, she was so sick of the never-ending struggle between her heart over her mind. Mind over heart. She wanted to be happy, but just didn't know how to get there.

She got to the front porch and leaned up against the old wood railing. She watched as he got to his feet, but did nothing to close the gap between them. A few months ago there'd been thousands of words she'd wanted to say. She'd had pretend conversations with him over and over until she was sick of hearing herself talk. Now, all the words seemed moot, and she couldn't for the life of her think of anything that needed to be said.

So she waited. She wouldn't make this easy. He'd been the one that had left. He'd be the one to speak first.

She could control her mouth, but apparently not her eyes. Her gaze flowed over him like hot fudge over ice cream. She took in how the baby blue of his gaze had darkened into something more intense. Sad, maybe? And how his long-unkempt hair that had been his trademark was now cut and neatly combed back into submission. His uniform was the same, black short-sleeved shirt showing off the tattoos that curled and emphasized his muscular arms, and a pair of jeans. The boots weren't at all ratty, but his guitar was. She recognized the instrument as the one he traveled with and wrote his songs on. She'd always wondered how long he'd had it.

"I wrote you a song." He spoke first. Good. She would've waited until hell froze over before she did.

She nodded. The song. The song had been hard to listen to and at the same time exactly what she needed to be able to heal. "I heard."

He arched a brow. How did such a simple gesture make her heart sigh with joy? "Really? How?"

She tilted her head to indicate the truck. "I heard the debut on the radio on the way home. Just tonight."

He nodded again, ending with a glance down at his boots. "I wasn't sure when they were going to release it. I wanted to get here to play it for you first, but it was probably for the best. I think I would've had a hard time making it all the way through without my voice breaking."

He found her gaze, his eyes darker and shinier than she remembered. A trick of the porch light? Maybe, but then again, he'd always been better about letting his true emotions show. He'd always been braver than she in that way. "It was a hard song to write; even harder to record. But I'm glad you heard it. I'm glad."

Why did she want to cry? Hadn't she done enough of that tonight already? It was so hard to look at him. He'd broken her heart, and then all of a sudden she knew exactly what she wanted to say. The words were so important, she couldn't look him in the eye in case he told her what she didn't want to hear.

She stuffed her hands in her pockets, turned her back, and stared out across the flat prairie of her land. She knew that past the stables and the training arena was a flat grassy stretch that went on for over a mile before breaking up against the slow-flowing creek. She couldn't see any of that now, not with the thick cover of the clouds and the soft fall of rain. "Is it true? Is what you said in the song all true, or did you make that up? I need to know."

She heard him shift his stance behind her and clear his throat, but she still wouldn't turn around. It was better if she concentrated on the things she could count on; things she knew for sure would always be there.

"Every word, DJ. Every word was true." His words were

like sparks from a match, each one burning as they reached her.

A flash of lightening lit up the sky, mirroring the anger that jolted through her.

He couldn't do this to her. He couldn't write a love song, show up on her front porch, and then expect her not to fall in love with him. What did he want from her? He wasn't playing fair. She'd let him go. She'd cut all ties, and now he was back, breaking all the rules.

But that was typical. Brent never cared two flying figs about rules. He'd always done what he damn well pleased. She turned to him then, arms crossed and in defense mode, jaw tight and eyes narrowed.

"What do you want from me? What am I supposed to do with that? With this?" She gestured her hand up and down to encompass everything about this situation—the song, his speech, him. "What do you want me to do now?"

He stepped toward her, then. She had every intention of moving back, keeping her distance, but she didn't want to back down.

She'd been good. Been strong enough, until he touched her arm. A hesitant touch of his fingers on her skin, and her body wanted to betray her and melt right into his arms. "DJ, please. Just hear me out."

Both of his hands were on her now, running up and down her arms as if warming her from the inside out. "What I said in the song was true. When... when we made love that night. I... I knew something had changed inside of me. I'd never been happier. I'd never felt like that with anyone. It was like we'd known each other forever. And you knew me, not the rock star, not the singer or even the artist, but just me, the man, Brent. I'd never had such a deep connection with anyone, never been so real or so honest. When I got up that day, there was this overwhelming sense of coming home and peace, and I knew I could stay here on this ranch with you forever."

She let herself drink in her last sight of him. He had stolen that right from her before, so she'd best to prepare her heart for her last look at him. "Then why? Why did you up and leave without a word?"

"That's what I'm trying to tell you. I got scared. I knew everything had changed, or at least that everything would change. I'd worked so long for my career. I thought I wanted fame and stardom, and then being here with you made all that seem frivolous and small. The thought of going back to that life was almost unbearable, and that scared me most of all, because I'd been chasing that life forever. Music had been my goal, my dream, and now my dream has changed because of you. Who was I if not Brent Kane, one of country music's superstars?"

She gritted her teeth and swallowed the lump in her throat. He took her hand and stroked each finger with his thumb, callused from years of plucking strings on his guitar. "How is it that all I do is sing all day long and you do hard labor and yet, your hands are the softest I've ever felt?"

She didn't care about her hands. She wanted him to continue the conversation. "Focus, Brent. You were saying?"

He smiled and brought her fingers up to his lips for a small kiss. "Right. I was saying I thought I could just leave and this feeling, this fear of everything changing, would go away. I could just go back to my old life, but..."

"But?"

"But it didn't work. I was miserable. I just kept thinking of this ranch, and Derrek, and most of all, of you. What you were doing? How you were holding up? If you missed me. If you even thought of me."

"What exactly are you saying, Brent?" Her voice tightly reined and controlled like a wild horse about to break free. "That you want to live here? What about your music?"

Pain flickered across his face, but he covered it well. "Writing and performing music is my life. It's who I am. But I realize that who I want to be is the man I am when I am with you. So, yes. Yes, I'm walking away. I'm ready, if you'll take me back."

She let her mouth drop open while she stared at him as if he'd lost his mind. "For one of the most talented men in country pop in our lifetime, you sure are a total idiot."

He stepped closer, squeezing her hands even more. "What, you don't want me back?"

"Brent, you don't have to choose." She shook her head. "It doesn't have to be one or the other. That's how things always are with you. Hot or cold. Completely obsessed or utterly uninterested. Just because you're here with me doesn't mean you have to give up your career. You can have both."

"Really? You're okay with that?" His eyes widened and his body relaxed, as if the weight of his death sentence had finally been pardoned.

She pulled her hands away, getting angry. "When have I ever said I wasn't okay with that? When have I ever asked you to choose?"

"When you told me that you needed a man as reliable as the rising sun. A man who was here with you every day. As a musician, I travel, I'm on tour. I can't be here and pursue my career at the same time."

She rolled her eyes. Idiot. "I meant that I needed someone I could always count on, that would be here if I needed him. That he'd make his home with me, not that I needed a freaking babysitter. Besides, after a few months, you'd drive me crazy. I'm used to working and living on this ranch alone, and I already have one man I have to take into consideration when making decisions. If I started having to take you into consideration as well, I'd probably kill you."

A sweet, lopsided grin worked its way to his mouth. "So, it might be best that I go on tour?"

She lost herself in his gaze. Forgot about her broken heart in his sexy smile, and spoke without thinking. "We'll work it out. Shorter trips are fine, and for longer ones I can go visit you. But yes, I want you to be happy, and I can't imagine you ever would be without music in your life."

His eyes lit up. The love she saw there was almost too much to take. "So what are you saying? Are you saying you'll take me back?"

Damn her. She'd gotten caught up again. When would she ever learn? She stepped away to get her bearings. No, that's not what she was saying, but it sure the hell had sounded like that's what she meant. Fear sprang up in her heart where joy had just tried to take root. "Brent, I don't know. This is crazy."

Too late, she could see Brent had taken her answer as a yes. He just wanted to convince her a bit more. Damn it, she should've been firmer. Taken a hard line with him. Told him to get the hell off her porch.

Brent broke into a wide smile. "Oh Love, I can work with, 'I don't know.' 'I don't know' just means you need a bit more information before you make your decision, and I've got all night. I can sweet talk you until you give up out of sheer exhaustion."

She turned her back on him again, more out of self-preservation than anger, but just as quickly went back to facing him—arms crossed, jaw set. She could not allow herself to get sucked in. It would be too simple. She was just not a woman who could love that easily.

"DJ, what do you need me to do to convince you? Because I've come prepared for all the grand gestures." In a heartbeat, he'd dropped to one knee in front of her and held up a tiny black box in one hand.

Fear like nothing she'd ever felt rushed through her. This was too fast, too quick. "Brent, I swear to God, if there's a ring in that box and you're about to propose then I will get my daddy's rifle and make you wish you were a sprinter and not a singer."

His face deadpanned, and with a toss of his hand, the ring box went flying out over the rail into the wet mud behind him. "What? There's no ring, and I'm only down on one knee because I thought your shoe lace was untied. I didn't want you to trip."

"I'm wearing boots."

"All the more reason I was concerned." He looked down and brushed a bit of mud off her boot. "But since everything looks good here, I'll just get back up."

He stood and DJ breathed in his unique scent of leather, soap, and the spicy cologne she could never quite guess.

"Please, DJ, I love you so much. Just give me one more chance. One more is all I ask, and I swear I'll spend the rest of my life making it up to you." He stood before her with love in his gaze and his heart on his sleeve. How could she not respect a man so willing to put himself out there, so willing to put his happiness in her hands?

She'd always known she was strong. Strong enough to survive her parents' death. Strong enough to run a ranch. Strong enough to not get her heart broken. But was she brave? Did she have the guts to fall in love again, no holding back, and give everything she had to this relationship?

She was. She smiled at Brent and nodded.

He kissed her then. Arms wrapped around her. Her fingers in his hair. Their mouths quickly doing away with the niceties and on to mimicking what their bodies wanted to do most. She felt herself give in. There was no point in fighting. Her heart had been his since she was fifteen, and there was no turning back now. The kiss only ended after both of their bodies were warmed and their breathing fast and short.

They stood on the porch looking out across the front lawn. The night was still ripe with clouds, but a full moon peeked through, sealing a promise of clear skies soon. Water dripped from the oak trees, and the clean scent of rain permeated the air. DJ rested her head on his shoulder, almost completely content with just having him near.

Almost.

"So, you curious at all?" he said, voice as casual as if asking what she had for breakfast this morning.

Dying.

She shrugged. "No. Nope, don't really care either way."

"No guesses on style? Shape? Number of... karats?" His natural Texas drawl on the last word the only indication of teasing.

She shook her head and grunted in a non-committal manner. The silence wobbled and was clumsy, like a drunken cowboy after drinking away his pay. She shifted her stance. Her right toe tapped inside her boot. "But, I mean... if you had a number in your head just floating around, and you wanted to say it that would be okay."

"Hmmm," he murmured, adjusted his hat. "So, just any old random number would do?"

Her gaze flitted to her boots, his boots, the porch chair railing. "No, just, I mean, if there was a specific number you were thinking about because... because that's what you were thinking."

"Do you like the number three?"

"Oh..." Her heart quickened, and her fingers floated to the base of her neck. "Oh, I like three. I mean, I think three is a good number."

"Oh, good." He nodded and gave her shoulder a quick squeeze. "I'm starving. How about I make you my famous cheese omelet for dinner? I promised Derrek that if he let me sit on the porch and wait for you, I'd feed him."

She nodded.

He turned and held the front door open for her. She looked up at him, his face giving nothing away. She smiled, then wiped her hands on her jeans and made her way inside.

———

Derrek looked up from where he was lounging on the couch and watched his sister walk through the door like a broomstick had been stuck down her pants and her jaw muscle was preparing to crack walnuts. He was concerned until he glanced at Brent, who smiled and gave him a telling wink. Apparently, his best friend had popped the big question to DJ and seemed overly confident in the answer. Brent had asked earlier for his blessing on marrying his sister. Derrek just shook his head and told him he wasn't the one Brent should be worried about. From the look on his sister's face, he'd been right.

Derrek watched DJ make her way into the kitchen, then stop and look around as if it were the first time she'd stepped foot in there. Both men waited, both gazes trained on her. Then, without any notice, she turned on Brent, mumbled something about him being a certain donkey's body part under her breath, and ran back out the front door like her hair was on fire.

Brent busted out laughing, but was quick to follow. Derrek groaned. Guess he'd have to go see if he was giving his best friend a congratulatory hug or a punch in the face. He got to his feet and walked outside. He was actually surprised at how little he was taken aback that his best friend was standing on the porch with a total Cheshire cat grin on his face while his sister was down on her hands and knees crawling around in the mud.

He stood and watched as DJ dug her hands through the mud, her hair streaming down her back, and clothes soaked through by the rain. Then he looked down at Brent's hand. He groaned. "I'm guessing that's what she's looking for."

Brent nodded.

Derrek rubbed his hand over his forehead and then pinched the bridge of his nose. "So how long are you gonna let her crawl around in the mud before you tell her you've had the ring this whole time?"

Brent shook his head. "I don't know, but her wanting to find the ring so badly is doing my heart good."

Derrek smothered a laugh behind his hand. "Oh, she's gonna be so pissed. You are a brave man, my friend. A brave man."

"Or stupid."

"I'll vote for that too. But I have to give it to you both, it sure won't be boring."

Brent looked over at him, his face beaming with a wide smile. "Oh, I'm counting on that."

Then he walked down the steps and fell to all fours beside DJ to help her "look" for the ring. Within a minute they were both covered in mud, soaking wet, and laughing like children.

"I found it!" Brent said, coming to his knees with a shiny diamond between his fingers and a silly grin on his face.

DJ slipped it on her finger and then grabbed Brent's face between her muddy hands and kissed him. They both went down in a fit of giggles, each struggling to get on top. "Welcome to the family, brother," Derrek shouted from the porch, pretty sure that neither of them were listening. "I wish you both the best."

After that, Derrek turned to go inside. It was one thing to watch one fool flail around in the mud, but two? Derrek shook his head and mumbled under his breath, "'Cause you're gonna need all the help you can get."

NINETEEN

*hree months later...*

DJ pulled her custom-painted, vanity-plated, Ford F-450 behind a black pick-up truck, threw her gear shift into park, and got out, slamming the truck door behind her. She'd been driving around the thick pine forest for over an hour now looking for some crappy, two-bit cabin, in the middle of Somewhere that apparently no one else could find. Well, no one else, but her and Chandler Sloan. She reached into the bed of her truck and pulled out the bull whip she put back there just for a little incentive. Some men seemed to respond better to threats than others.

She maneuvered her way through the dense forest, making her way around the tall, anorexic trees with their needle-like fingers scratching at the blue sky as if grappling for the last bit of sunlight. The one thing that Somewhere had plenty of was pine, and since one damn tree looked like another, it had taken her way too long to find the right turn off. It wasn't as if she was one of the VonBrandts—whose abundance of wealth only seemed surpassed by their unlimited amount of time—and knew every acre of this forest like it was tattooed on the black side of their eyelids.

Of course, none of them had the Double D horse ranch to run. But she did, which was why she didn't have time to be playing these hide and seek games with the oldest son of one of the town's most well-to do families—freaking Chandler Sloan.

The memory came grating back of a soft voice on the other end of her phone, and how even the smooth, southern accent couldn't cover the worry floating over the air waves. "I can't find him, DJ," Ellie Sloan said, in her *Gone With The Wind* dialect that only women of a certain stature and age could get away with. "The funeral is tomorrow, and he's been gone for close to three days. You're the only one I know who can find him and make him come home."

Make Chandler Sloan do anything her ass.

If DJ knew Chandler at all it was that the only reason he'd *ever* give up the comforts of his multi-million dollar ranch and hole up in the two-bit hunting shed was so he could hide out and drink himself sick. She just hoped he'd gone through most of the liquor by now and was swinging the pendulum back to somewhat sober.

DJ hiked her way up and stood in front of the rotted out cabin that seemed to lean heavily with its own variety of weather-beaten intoxication. And if its halfway hanging door, and sad-smiling roof wasn't enough, the one and only window looked as if a raccoon had done something obscene against the glass pane. She settled her hat down further, and then dusted off her hands on her work jeans. She hadn't bothered to wash up, pretty sure after a weekend of binge drinking, Chandler wouldn't be sporting his Sunday best.

Best to get this over with. Not going to be pleasant no matter how long she procrastinated, and with her new filly being delivered later today, there'd be no way she'd miss that just because Chandler Sloan was angry at the world —again.

Seemed like the man had spent half his life pissed off over one thing or another. Hell, she couldn't have been the only one to fantasize about tripping him on a long walk over a short pier or playing a very intense game of hangman with a noose and a tree.

But "pretty" covered a multitude of sins and the mayor liked the Sloans' tax bracket, so Chandler was tolerated. And that's why his momma had called *her*. Not her brother and once-upon-a-time Chandler's best-friend, Derrek Diaz , not her fiancé and long ago Chandler's childhood friend, Brent, but *her,* because the damn prick had alienated most of his friends and turned the rest into enemies.

How they were still on speaking terms, she had no idea. Guess she had a soft spot for lost causes and hot-headed cowboys. She stomped over to the cabin door and pushed it open—no need to knock when there was no way he'd be in a position to answer.

The sunlight shot in like a bullet, tearing through any hope she had of finding Chandler sober. The stench came next, punching her in the face—the waves of tequila and sweat so strong her eyes watered.

But find him she did. There he was, flat out on a rickety, iron-framed bed in the corner, groaning and batting at the sunlight like a washed up boxer inside a nightmare.

"What the fu—" His curse got lost along with his

balance as he toppled over and fell face first onto the dirty wooden floor.

"Good God, Chandler, this place reeks." DJ wandered in, carefully lifting a half empty beer bottle from off a wooden chair she now thought better of occupying.

"If you don't like it then leave." Chandler growled, but at least he was sober enough to push himself into a sitting-slouched position instead of staying face first on the floor. She'd take that as a good sign.

She'd take anything as a good sign at this point.

DJ assessed the damage. This was not the man Chandler showed to the world—neat, freshly starched button-up, creased jeans, highly polished, hundred dollar black boots. Nope, this Chandler was a mess. Thick black whiskers dusted his cheeks and neck. His hair was a greasy mess with one side matted to his skull and the other sticking in every direction but down. His shirt, with wrinkles the size of pleats and sweat-rings the size of doughnuts, hadn't fared the binge drinking any better.

A person would never guess he was one of the town's most eligible bachelors. He'd just as easily be mistaken for the homeless vet that wandered the downtown area eating out of trash cans and shaking his fist at God.

It really was hard to feel bad for Chandler. He had everything going for him: looks, money, an IQ in the genius range, and one of the state's top ranches as a family business. He'd been lucky in everything except love. And if it hadn't been because of that one thing, DJ would've screwed the guilt Ellie Sloan was a master at slinging her way, and left Chandler to his own devices.

Except DJ did know. She knew what had happened to Chandler when he'd been young and in love. She'd sat with him more than once in a dark corner at Everyday Joe's, and had seen behind the sharp cutting barbs and sarcastic pompous attitude. The pain in his voice and the memory of how he used to be was enough for her to find some compassion in her heart and cut him some slack.

That, and oh yeah, because his dad had just died.

One would think she'd have a little more sympathy seeing that both of her parents had died when she was fifteen, but then she knew the real reason Chandler was taking to the bottle like some ranch hand new to whoring.

"We can do this the hard way or the easy way," DJ said, trying to calculate how much time it would take to get him up and moving. "But either way you're getting up and gonna do it in a quick manner because you're wasting my time."

"What the hell is that supposed to mean?" Chandler spat out, doing his best to hold her gaze through his blood shot eyes.

She *so* did not need this right now. She had guests coming in from all over the country, a wedding the size of a presidential inauguration to prepare for, and a ranch that she'd been forced to stop micromanaging. Her patience was wearing thin. "It means that I will gladly use whatever means necessary." She tapped the leather whip against her leg, not feeling at all bad when Chandler's eyes widened at the gesture. "Or you can get up on your own and go get a shower and a change of clothes, because you've got company and the funeral is tomorrow. Pity party is over."

"If a man can't have a few drinks in memory of his dead father then when can he?" Chandler tripped to his feet, but then landed flat back out on the bed. At least this time he was semi propped up against the wall.

Progress. At this rate she should be home in time to see

her unborn children go off to college. Apparently, a pity party couldn't be called a party unless more than one person was involved. Resigned, she took her life into her own hands, and tested her weight on the rickety hard back chair. "We both know that's not really why you're here killing off brain cells at such a rapid rate that I'm in fear for your literacy level."

"What?" Chandler rubbed at his eyes as if sand was in them. "I don't even know what the hell you're saying."

"I'm too late then." She sighed and shook her head. And this man had gone to Harvard, unbelievable. Some things never changed, like the fact that DJ and he acted more like brother and sister than friends, and that they'd had this conversation more than once. Good thing she had nothing better to do... like go to her last wedding dress fitting, review the seating arrangements, approve the freaking table settings for the umpteenth time. DJ eyed a half empty bottle of beer on the floor and wondered how many of those she'd have to drink to stay up here and hide out for the rest of the week.

"Look," DJ said, trying the more sympathetic route. "I'm sorry about your father. I know that you had a..." She searched for the right word. Not finding one, did the best she could. "Complex relationship with him. So I'm confident his passing away was not what drove you up here trying your best to get placed on the liver transplant list."

"Guess I won't hold my breath waiting for you to donate." Chandler whined, his chin already falling to his chest.

DJ let her eyes close for half a beat. When the pity party was in full swing, there wasn't much that could be done except crash the damn thing. "At this point I'm not even willing to give you the kick in the pants you so desperately need, but..." She stood, took a deep breath, and dove head first into the waves of stench. "I promised your mother, so..."

DJ grabbed him by the arm and pulled. He was heavier than he looked. All solid muscle underneath the homeless man exterior.

He growled at her, but made it to his feet. He held his head with both hands and stumbled toward the front door, kicking over empty beer bottles along the way.

DJ propped him up with her shoulder, and stumbled down the small hill, making their way to her truck. Once there, she reached inside the front seat, and pulled out a bottle of water.

Chandler opened it, downing the entire contents in one gulp, then wiped his mouth and muttered a thank you. Then he dug at his eyes with his palms and winced. "God, your truck makes my head hurt."

DJ reached over and patted the hood of her Ford F-450, with its decked out chrome wheels and custom paint job. Her outrageously *gorgeous* pink truck was the envy of every cowgirl in Somewhere.

Yeah, it's that awesome.

"You're just jealous because my truck is happy. My truck is fun. When people see us coming they smile. When they see you coming they cower. Your truck's nothing to get excited about, just plain, boring, black—the same color as the lump of coal you carry in place of your heart."

Chandler grunted or it may've been a laugh—hard to tell with him. "So, you're telling me I'm black hearted."

"Or no hearted. Take your pick."

He peeled back a lid and eyeballed her up and down as if finally noticing who the hell had shot through his cabin door to drag him back home. His expression was shelter-puppy pathetic, his blue-gray eyes anything but.

"Why didn't I fall in love with you—a woman with a heart —a pink heart? Shoulda married you when I had the chance."

DJ looked up at the sky—pretty blue, nice fat white clouds reminding her of cupcakes, cream puffs... and a dead man under the heel of her boot 'cuz she'd rather hack off her leg and eat her own foot then have ever married Chandler Sloan.

"Guess by the size of the ring on your finger, I'm too late even for that." Chandler grumbled, slouching against her truck as if she didn't have her wedding to get ready for, and he didn't have his father's funeral to attend. Really? She had no time to travel down this particular rabbit hole...again.

This isn't the first time Chandler has had this particular drunken flight of fancy, but every time come morning, sanity returns and he remembers there's never been anything between them except brotherly affection.

DJ suppressed a growl of her own, and then opened the driver's side door, hoping he'd take the hint. "Yeah, Brent proposed, dumb ass. I seemed to have missed your congratulations."

Maybe she was still a little bitter that she hadn't heard a word from Chandler once she'd gotten engaged. She thought she would've at least rated a text message, but Chandler was notorious for his dark brooding silences. She shouldn't have expected anything more.

"More like condolences," Chandler said, letting his head rest back against the truck and his hands fall down by his side. For a second DJ thought he might've fallen asleep. "Brent's no good for you. You could've done so much better."

"Better, meaning you?" DJ laughed. Only a condescending prick like Chandler would think marrying the love of her life and country singer who was up for a Grammy was below her. "Really? Because we both know there's only ever been Jayne for you."

There might've been a brief period of time after Brent had left to follow his dream in L.A. that she'd thought of Chandler as more than just a friend. But it hadn't taken long for her to realize that whatever was left of Chandler's heart, had and always would, belong to Jayne.

He was silent. Typical. But he was the one who'd started it and she wasn't letting him out of it easily. "Are we going to talk about what this whole childish episode was about, or are we going to pretend there's nothing wrong?"

"I've no idea what you mean."

Pretending it is, then. "So, is she expected to be here for the funeral?"

Chandler crossed his arms and stared straight ahead. That was "yes" in Sloan speak.

"And this will be the first time Jayne will have been back since…?"

His eyes popped open and spine straightened—nothing like the mention of Jayne to get his blood pumping. "Since she left nine years ago. Yes, yes I'm well aware of who's coming to stay in my damn house like she's some kinda prodigal returning home."

"She did grow up there. It's her childhood home." DJ couldn't help but poke the bear. It was payback for cutting into her day.

"Not her home now."

DJ voiced a loud humph, and then pulled herself up into her truck. She almost felt sorry for Jayne. Almost. The raw deal she'd given him all those years ago had left Chandler broken and bitter, and he'd never recovered. If someone had cared about her opinion, DJ would've said that Jayne was directly responsible for the man Chandler had become.

And unfortunately that man was a full out prick.

Thank you so much for reading ROCK STAR! I hope you enjoyed the antics of both Brent and DJ, but the story isn't over.

The biggest wedding Somewhere, Texas has ever seen is in the works, but that's not what's occupying DJ's time. When the most eligible bachelor in all of Somewhere goes missing, DJ is the one who gets roped in to bringing Chandler Sloan back home.

Chandler Sloan has everything, money, power, and heart-stopping good looks, except Jayne, the one woman who betrayed him and the only woman he's ever loved.

But there's more to Jayne than meets the eye, and soon both will realize the only thing blacker than Chandler's heart... is Jayne's secrets.

Download BLACKHEARTED right now!

BLACKHEARTED

Excerpt

Laughter floated out from the living room and down the hallway, rubbing him wrong like sandpaper would cotton. He bristled, his foul mood not at all consoled by someone else's joyous one. The muscles in his jaw tightened. His teeth doing their best to flatten against each other.

He walked into the seating area and came smack up against a voice that caused a rush of memories to flood his brain, and long dead emotions to fill his heart. Chandler reached out and leaned against the wall to allow the wave of dizziness to pass and let his heart find its familiar cold, black rhythm.

He took in the scene before him. To his right was his mother, sitting in a low-backed loveseat whose weepy smile made his head hurt, next to her was his sister, Dixie, whose laugh had been the one that tripped down the hallway. Across from them was his twin brother, Tatum, whose casual one-arm placement around the back of the couch behind Jayne fooled no one.

Especially him.

But none of them mattered. Not right now. Because Chandler had eyes only for one person in that room. One person whose slender shoulders and long neck seemed stiff and too formal. Whose dark, thick hair was pulled up into a tight bun making her look years older than she should. Whose full lips seemed as foreign to a smile as a winter storm in the desert and whose hazel eyes reminded him of two copper pennies that long ago lost their shine—dirty and cheaply used.

Jayne.

How long since he'd given up on ever seeing her in his house again? How long since he'd stopped wanting her to come? He must've made a noise, or hell sucked all the joy out of the room by his mere presence, since everyone in the room stopped talking and looked up.

He felt their stares, everyone's stares, but he only cared about one. She looked different, a stranger almost. More than just the passing of years. If he hadn't spent days studying her face in every shade of light, if he hadn't spent hours watching how the sun set her hair to glowing, or how her skin looked mocha soft next to his own, he might've passed her in the street without even recognizing her.

But he had.

Her gaze stayed locked with his as if she too was having a hard time taking in how he'd changed. He knew what she saw. If looking in the mirror wasn't enough, he had his twin brother's face to remind him how much more the years had marked his own. Where Tatum's face showed faint laugh lines at the corner of his eyes, and his mouth found the upturned angle of a smile with ease, Chandler's eyes were devoid of lines of happiness and his mouth had settled into the same flat line of disapproval that his father had modeled so well.

His mother stood, a kind smile reaching her eyes. No black widow's weeds for her. No puffy eyes or pale, heartbroken face. No, his mother was all in summer-white, with a long silver necklace that ended at her trim waist, and French manicured nails that emphasized the large diamond rock his father had given her on their twentieth anniversary.

"You're home? Her voice flitted upward as if she didn't quite believe he was standing in front of her.

What? She was surprised? As if she hadn't been the one who'd called DJ to come fetch him home. But someone had to break the silence. It was getting awkward, even for him. He lifted a shoulder. "Thought I would come in and see what all the laughter was about. Didn't think there was a cause for celebration."

Out of the corner of his eye, he watched his sister pinch the bridge of her nose and shake her head.

Yep, this was happening, and yeah he was getting ready to be a total douche. Deal with it.

He walked over and threw himself into the chaise lounge, not caring at all that his mother grimaced as he propped up his dirty boots on her white furniture. She was the one who'd insisted on upholstering everything in white on a working cattle ranch. Tatum, seemingly sensing Chandler's mood, removed his arm from the back of Jayne's chair and rubbed his neck. Good—because Chandler was about to rip it out of its socket.

"Soooo, Jayne just got here." Dixie said, following their mom's lead of trying to fill the silence.

Way to state the obvious, Dix. Not like he'd taken his eyes off her since he'd walked into the room.

If Jayne was uncomfortable with his attention, she didn't show it. There was no fidgeting, no defiant tilt of her chin. No foul word off her lush, ample mouth or narrowed gaze to call him on his crap. No, she just sat there and took it with the tranquility of a yoga master who'd found his center. Took his gaze, ignoring the anger that blazed off of him, and acted as if he were no more annoying than a buzzing fly on a summer's picnic

Tatum cleared his throat. "Well, we were just talking about the—" he broke off and coughed into his hand. "Bro, what is that smell? Is that you? Where the hell have you been?"

"Drinking," Chandler said, gaze locked onto Jayne's face as if equipped with heat-seeking-technology.

"Lord knows it smells like it." Tatum winced.

"And I think I'll have another," Chandler added just to be a dick.

"Riiight," Tatum drew out in an exaggerated sigh. "Because that's going to make this whole situation a lot better."

"Oh my goodness, refreshments. What was I thinking?" His mom grasped at the social nicety with relish. She turned toward Jayne. "Honey, what would you like to drink? I have some sweet tea, or that flavored sparkling water you liked, or perhaps you'd like something stronger. A Vodka and tonic maybe? I find we all handle Chandler better after one or two of those."

His mom's question was just the thing to break the trance Jayne had been in. She turned her whole body away from him, effectively cutting him off with the sharp snip of her shoulders. There was no way he'd not take that personally. "No, no Ellie," Jayne said. "Please, I got this. I don't want you to wait on me. I'm here to take care of you, not the other way around."

"Oh, and here, I thought you were just back for the money," Chandler said. *Don't turn your back on me.*

"Chandler!" his mother snapped at him. "This is still my house, and Jayne is a guest here. I will not tolerate that kind of rudeness. Apologize."

But Jayne shook her head; saving him from having to ask for forgiveness, which was good since he didn't think he could choke the words out. "It's okay. We are all under a lot of stress. But I'll take this as a cue to go and get the drinks. I've been sitting the whole time in the car, and I need to stretch my legs."

She stood and smoothed her black, pinstriped dress pants that ended above a pair of old lady flats and then did a straightening tug on a white, button up shirt with its only nod toward frilliness, a slightly embellished collar. He hated her clothes. The outfit reminded him of a waitress, or worse, a servant. Where had the girl gone who loved soft plaid shirts and wore jeans like she was poured into them? Who pulled on a pair of worn boots and a straw cowboy hat and was good to go all day? He guessed a lot of things had changed.

Chandler watched her walk out of the living room and

turn the corner into the kitchen. It would be a bad idea to follow her. The worst idea ever, and yet, there were two seconds, total, before he was on his feet pursuing her out the door.

"Chandler, don't!" Dixie's shout punched him in the back, but he barely noticed. He had the taste of blood in his mouth and was damn well sick of swallowing it.

Want more? Download BLACKHEARTED right now!

Continue reading for another sneak peek at the book that started it all, *Texas Wide Open*.

"A tortured hero, a love that defies distance and time...this is a book you won't soon forget." Cat Johnson

He did the unforgivable to make her leave. Now it's going to take a heart the size of Texas to make her love him again.
Download the book that started it all—TEXAS WIDE OPEN—now!

Katie always knew she'd marry Cole one day—until he broke her dreams and her heart. But now that Katie's father is sick, she's back home, older, wiser and nowhere near the love-sick fool she once was.

Cole knows Katie doesn't want anything to do with him. But after so many years, he can't pretend she's no more than a neighbor. Holding his ground was hard enough when she was seventeen. Now that she's her own woman, Cole's heart doesn't stand a chance...

"Passionate, gritty and fast paced...with a hot blooded, honorable hero to make every woman's knees go weak." Diane Whiteside

Download TEXAS WIDE OPEN now or continue reading for a sneak peek at the story that started it all.

TEXAS WIDE OPEN

*K*atie slouched on the peeling wood steps that led to the back porch. With elbows firmly propped up on knees, she dropped her chin into her hands. Everyone else was inside talking in hushed tones, eating rolled up meat and dried crackers with white goo on them.

Her stomach growled. The "finger sandwiches," which didn't look like fingers at all, were real small and not one of them had peanut butter and jelly in them. She could've complained to Pa. He would've found her something good to eat, but she was still mad at him.

Pa had made her wear the yellow dress that had ruffles around the neck, the one that choked and itched. She *hated* that dress. It made her look like a baby and at eight years old, she was no baby.

How was Cole supposed to know that she was a big girl if Pa dressed her all stupid like? But Katie had seen the look on her father's face, and learned there was no arguing when his mouth got all tight and small like that.

Still, she'd won one battle. She raised one foot to peek at the scuffed leather boot. Yep, her most favorite shoes in the whole world—her pink boots. She'd waited 'til the last minute so there'd been no time for Pa to send her back to change or else they'd miss the you-la-gee, whatever that was. So she wore her pink cowgirl boots, and had flashed her prettiest smile every time one of the 'dults told her that she sure did look cute.

In the end, wearing them wasn't worth the trouble she'd get later, cuz the one person who shoulda noticed, didn't. Cole.

Katie hugged herself and rocked slightly, her stomach still fluttery from when Pa had nudged her to walk to the front of the church where Cole, his sister, Nikki, and his ma had stood. Katie's stomach did that a lot when she saw Cole. His dark hair had grown shaggy, and she loved how it fell to one side. She loved his blue eyes that always made her think of the Texas sky and how his crooked smile made her smile. He was eight years older, almost grown, but he'd never treated her like a baby. Which was cool, because sometimes even Pa did that.

Most of the time when she saw him, she'd throw herself into his arms, and he'd always give her a hug and twirl her 'round and 'round 'til Pa would tell them to settle down. But today was different. Today, she felt terrible. Cole, her best friend, her cowboy, was sad.

Katie had walked up to Cole's mom after the funeral, not sure what to do. Mrs. Logan had been a mess. Her hair wasn't smoothed back into a tight bun like usual, but fuzzy. She had shivered inside her black sweater, which was odd since Katie's dumb dress was already stuck to her. There was one second when Katie didn't want to hug Mrs. Logan, afraid she'd knock her over. Then Cole's mom turned her lips into a half smile and Katie threw her arms around her, burying her nose in the smell of fabric softener and maple syrup.

"Ah Katie, my breath of fresh air," she said, patting Katie's head. "You need to help Cole. Be there for him."

Katie had nodded. But when she'd hugged Cole with all her strength, he just stood there, not saying one word. Even when she mumbled "sorry" like everyone else had, he hadn't looked at her. Nope, just stared straight ahead like he was picturing himself somewhere else and not at the church at all.

Nikki as usual, had never looked at her. Katie shrugged. Nikki was older, almost ten, and she didn't play with babies. At least that was what Nikki had told Katie the last time she'd gone over looking for Cole. That was fine with Katie. Nikki was boring anyway. All she cared about was that beat-up, old pool table the Logans had out back. She didn't care about horses. Not like Katie did.

Katie heaved her shoulders and slumped even further. She peeled a blue paint chip off the worn step and held it up against the bright sky. Nope. Not quite. Her Pa always told her there was nothing quite as blue and quite as wide as the Texas sky. And Pa was always right. There wasn't a color blue she'd seen that matched the best sky in the whole world. Well, except the blue of Cole's eyes, and she wasn't going tell anyone that.

Katie flicked the paint chip to the ground and looked out past the giant oak tree. There in the distance was a two-rail wooden fence Cole's dad had just put up. In the holding area were the new horses that arrived only a few weeks ago. One of the horses, Cole told her, was pregnant and soon the first foal would be born to the Logans' Horse Ranch.

She'd heard one of the 'dults, Mike Pitt, talking about

how the horses had killed Cole's dad. He'd been real upset and had gone on about how Cole's dad shoulda known better. And about how the horses had cost lots of money and the stress on Cole's dad's heart was too much. Katie didn't understand and wanted to ask Mr. Mike how the horses could be to blame when Cole's dad died in his bed. But Katie couldn't because for some reason Pa didn't like her talking to him.

But Mr. Mike was wrong. It couldn't have been the horses. Seemed to her it was the sleepin' that had killed Cole's dad. He went to sleep and plumb forgot how to wake up. That's why from now on when she went to sleep she'd keep the bathroom light on, so she'd remember how to get up in the mornings.

One of the ponies neighed in greeting as Cole and her Pa went toward the fence. Her Pa had his arm around Cole's shoulder and was walking real slow. Funny, Cole always seemed so big to her, but next to Pa he didn't. Maybe cuz of the way his shoulders slumped and how his head hung down like he wanted to study the design on his black boots.

Pa lifted his hat and smoothed his hair. He had a habit of fiddling with his hat when a horse was having a hard time birthing a foal or when Katie got a note home from her teacher. So Katie sat real still and quiet so she could figure out what bothered Pa because next to him, Cole was her favorite person in the world.

Pa focused hard on Cole. His head bent low to Cole's dark one. Cole nodded, swiped at his eyes, and nodded again. Then Pa did something she'd never seen him do. Well, to anyone else except her. He hugged Cole. And not just a one-arm hug, but a real, both-arms-wrapped-around-and-squeezing, making-you-feel-all-safe-and-better kinda hug. And for one heartbeat, jealousy rolled through her. But it was gone just as quick because this was Cole who Pa hugged. And if Pa was going to hug anyone else, then it might as well be Cole because she knew a secret.

It was so secret she hadn't even told Pa. So secret she'd only whisper it at night and then only into her pillow. She was gonna marry Cole one day.

CHAPTER 1

CHAPTER 1

Thirteen years later, present day

Katie mentally prepared herself for the smells of antiseptic and bleach as she pushed through the double glass doors, but the hospital lobby surprised her. A floral arrangement on the reception desk brightened the space, giving off the scent of jasmine, and the darkened lights of the gift shop toned down the fluorescent glare from above.

The cheery, if somewhat outdated, mauve chairs sat empty and no one tended the front desk. Not much of a surprise since visiting hours had long passed and only loved ones desperate for miracles or updates would roam the halls at this hour.

Katie wheeled her suitcase behind her, glad she had only one bag. She'd packed light, knowing she'd come here straight from the airport. She patted down her coat and found her phone in the side pocket. Even in the deep of winter, south Texas didn't call for wool, but New York had been spitting gray and sleet when she'd left. Besides, her bones were still chilled from the early morning phone call.

She'd been dead to the world when her phone screeched its annoying ring tone. Half asleep, she'd answered. If she lived to be ninety she'd never forget the way Cole had said her name—as if on a tail end of a sigh. Her mind woke before her body, and she'd literally fallen out of bed. Now, as she touched the screen on her phone, she braced herself for the husky hello on the other end.

It was acceptable to be shocked by a middle-of-the-night phone call, that was something she could live with, but now, having had time to prepare, there was no excuse. Her stomach flopped around like a girl's first trip to the backseat of her boyfriend's car at the sound of Cole's hello.

"I'm here. What room are you in?" She was glad her voice sounded calm, almost bored. That was exactly the impression she was going for—at least with him.

He quickly told her the room number and which floor to get off on.

"See you in a minute then," she said, glad to get off the phone. She had no illusions her calm demeanor could withstand long conversations with Cole, especially when all she should be thinking about was Pa. She grabbed her suitcase and headed toward the main elevators. Stepping inside, she pushed the button for five and took a deep breath as she watched the digital numbers begin their upward count.

She pressed the palm of her hand flat under her breastbone to ease the tightness.

Had it always been this bad?

If she were a good daughter, she'd be worried about Pa. Worried about his surgery tomorrow, worried if he'd even make it out of the hospital. But instead her mind flashed on a time long past with a different man and one very scared horse.

She fished in her front jeans pocket, found her Chap-

Stick and then whipped on some cherry lip balm. She was such a fool. It had been close to three years and still her breath hitched at the thought of being in the same room as Cole.

Three years couldn't negate a lifetime of bad habits.

Katie closed her eyes and massaged back the headache that threatened. Apparently, three years wasn't long enough.

No, this wasn't about Cole and her. This was about Pa. And it was high time she remembered that Cole had been nothing but a passing fancy in a young girl's heart.

Download TEXAS WIDE OPEN now!

This rockstar's lost his muse and *her*. But now he's back and it's going to take a lot more than good looks and playboy charm to convince this cowgirl he's worth a second chance.

Download ROCK STAR now!

He bought her, but that doesn't mean she's his.

In a dystopian world where women are few and men need wives to hold land, Hudson pays an exuberant price to purchase the most beautiful woman he's ever seen.

But there's dangerous secrets his new wife is hiding, and it will take more than money—possibly his very life—to keep her.

Start the first book in this exciting, multi-award winning series today.

Download AS DUSK FALLS now!

Get both of these ebooks *free* just for signing up for my newsletter, and stay up to date on all my latest releases and book news.

FREE BOOKS HERE

ABOUT THE AUTHOR

KC Klein is award winning dystopian and sci-fi romance author. A Reader's Choice award, Prism award, and a prestigious RONE award, and two times RONE nominee, KC has published over thirteen books, both as an indie author, and with major New York publishing houses like Harper Collins and Kensington. She's been represented by both Nancy Yost Literary Agency and the Marsal Lyon Agency. She lives in sunny Arizona with one overly-indulgent husband, a couple of sarcastic teenagers, and two very spoiled dogs.

KC loves to hear from readers and can be found desperately pounding away on her laptop in yoga pants and leopard slippers or more conveniently at www.kckleinbooks.com. Join her Rock Star Facebook Fan Group for updates on her latest releases, sales, and ARC giveaways.

Receive a FREE book just for subscribing to my NEWSLETTER!

www.kckleinbooks.com

OTHER BOOKS BY KC KLEIN

Other Books by Series and all Platforms

Dark Future Series

As Dusk Falls

As Night Reigns

As Dawn Breaks

Dark Future Series Collection (books 1-3)

The Omega Galaxy Series

The Space Captain's Courtesan

In The Heart of Texas Series

Rock Star

Blackhearted

Lonesome

Wrong

New Adult Contemporary Box Set

Texas Fever series

Texas Wide Open

Hustlin' Texas

Married to the Mob Series (A Texas Fever series spin-off.)

Mi Familia: Part I

Mi Familia: Part II

Mi Familia: Part III

Mi Familia: Complete Box Set

Non-fiction

Journaling Your Way to a Novel in a Month: The Perfect NanoWriMo Companion

Dream Believe Write: Writing Prompts for Fiction Writers